Br
Dawn

Bright
Dawn

Jenny Robertson

Scripture Union
130 City Road, London EC1V 2NJ

Other Swift Books by Jenny Robertson
A Part to Play
Dark Journey
Light Sentence

© Jenny Robertson 1989
First published 1989

ISBN 0 86201 555 3

Phototypeset by INPUT Typesetting Ltd., London
Printed and bound in Great Britain by Cox and Wyman Ltd, Reading

Contents

This book completes the story of Stefan, told in *Dark Journey* and *Light Sentence*.
Koravia is a fictitious country but the people and events of this book are based on real happenings.

1

Flame before day

It was still dark when Stefan woke up. Everyone else in the hut was asleep. Stefan groped for the door, anxious not to disturb the others. Someone muttered in his sleep and Stefan paused, but today was Sunday. No need to get up. Even the informers who kept a lookout for trouble would roll over in their bunks and snatch some more hours of fitful sleep.

The door creaked open. Freezing air cut through Stefan's thin clothes. He felt his insides shudder, and he huddled his arms around him as he slithered over the snow towards a patch of frozen pines which lay within the barbed wire compound of the prison camp where he had spent the last fifteen months.

Searchlights swept across the black shapes of square watch towers which shut the prison camp off from the main building site where half finished factories and apartment blocks rose out of sheer mountainsides. Stefan ducked low, glad that his route was out of range of those questing lights.

The only light I've got is the end of a candle . . .

The end of a candle, which Stefan was going to light for his friends this Easter morning.

'Live the light,' the ploughman Adam Puls had urged Stefan.

'Live the light,' Michael Laski had begged, 'however hard it is for you there in the mountains . . .'

Adam, the gentle, visionary ploughman from the next village to Stefan's, had been locked away in a special mental hospital for violent criminals, immobilised day and night in drug-induced stupor, while Michael, who had already spent so many years in prison, was now serving a five year sentence doing hard labour in a coalmine.

Would Michael be keeping Easter in coaldust and darkness?

It was Easter when we first met, Stefan recalled; and his thoughts formed a prayer: Lord, may someone give Michael an Easter greeting and bring him happiness today!

This prayer seemed as weak as the slip of moon beyond the searchlights but it would be echoed, Stefan knew, by Helen, Michael's wife, caring for Nikolai, the baby son Michael had hardly seen, and by Martha, who loved all four of them: Helen, Michael, baby Nikolai and Stefan. Her letters to him rustled as Stefan searched through his pocket to find a match for his candle.

Stefan's prayer for Michael would be echoed too by people abroad who were becoming increasingly interested in life in his closed homeland, Koravia; not least the life of people like him who found that God was real although the leaders of Koravia had declared that religion was obsolete in their land-locked, one-party state.

It would be echoed most certainly by Andrey whose footsteps scrunched across frozen earth as he came towards the clump of scraggy trees to share Stefan's Easter vigil.

'Sorry I'm late: I couldn't find my jacket in the dark.'

'I slept in mine,' Stefan confessed.

'I can see you know how things are done in prison.' Andrey stuffed his fur cap into his pocket and pulled out his most precious possession. Both of them had sat out their time in punishment cells on starvation rations in an effort to keep the copy of the New Testament which Andrey opened.

Ankle deep in snow, they repeated traditional Easter anthems which would be sung all over Koravia: *We rise at deep dawn to welcome our joy*.

A guard dog howled from beyond the barbed wire.

Stefan bent forward and put a carefully hoarded match to his candle. The flame guttered then leapt up. He turned to Andrey with the Easter greeting:

'Alleluia, Christ is risen.'

'Christ has really risen,' Andrey replied, and they hugged each other, exchanging the customary three-fold embrace. Andrey opened his New Testament. Stefan held the candle close to the page, and with its flame and help from the lights around the perimeter fence they read the resurrection story as the sun rose behind the sleeping building-site and filled ravaged valleys with light. Then Andrey and Stefan brewed tea in the deserted camp kitchen and shared a piece of black bread.

'I'm glad we managed to get up early,' Andrey said. 'You know, I was thinking back to that time we first met. As soon as they got me inside the gates they body-searched me in front of the whole camp and took my Bible. I noticed the look on your face. I knew at once, that guy's one of us.' Andrey reached for the kettle. 'There's no more tea but we can top up with hot water.'

'Fine,' Stefan smothered a yawn. 'Yes, it was bad when they did that, but at least it meant we met up your very first moment inside.'

'They do what they can to intimidate us but the support we give one another keeps us surviving,' Andrey said. 'I've still got eighteen months to go, ten more than you, but of course you've been here for well over a year already.'

Stefan nodded. He looked across at his friend. It was Andrey's first prison sentence, but he'd been prepared for it by all the preliminaries Stefan himself knew so well: being reported, interviewed by the police, followed, searched, arrested, imprisoned, tried, sentenced – and all this in spite of talks from Party leaders that new possibilities for freedom of thought were developing in their country, although the government completely controlled the media, and the printing of dissenting literature, including Bibles, was banned.

'You were well known to me, of course,' Andrey went

on. 'At first you were just a name, a prisoner I prayed for. I guess I felt drawn to you because you're so young: almost five years younger than me. I was a student – I should have graduated by now if things had been different, but you know far more than me about suffering for your faith,' he added as they gathered up the kettle and metal mugs and sluiced them out in the sink.

'We'd better be going,' Andrey said. 'See you later – and thanks.'

He didn't have to say what for. Stefan understood.

That was nice of Andrey, saying all that, he thought, as he made his way through the early morning sunlight to his hut. He wished he'd found words to say encouraging things in return.

Still, the important thing is that we're in this together, he thought. Praying together like we do keeps us surviving.

Martha's letters kept Stefan surviving too, but her last one bothered him. He pulled it out and wrapped himself round with his blanket as he read it.

Stefan, I love you.

Martha's dark eyes smiled beyond the page. He took out her photographs. There she was, holding Michael and Helen's baby, Nikolai, against a background of summer sun and the lime trees which gave their village, Lipa, its name. That must have been taken almost a year ago; yes, there on the back in handwriting which Martha had got used to fitting into small spaces: *Niki and me just after his first birthday.*

And here was a winter one with Martha and Niki muffled up against the cold. He could see how much his little godson had grown, but he couldn't see enough of Martha. He looked again at the summer one, noticing the outline of Martha's figure, with Niki's plump bare legs crumpling her dress.

Martha, I love you too! How I wish you were here beside me so that I could tell you so! He kissed her photograph instead, cold and shiny beneath his chapped lips, and, huddled into his coarse blanket, Stefan gave

12

way to longing for a long moment before he put the photograph down and turned back to Martha's letter again.

In your first letters to me you worried whether I would wait two whole years for you. Of course I'll wait, but I am wondering whether we shouldn't get married while you're still in prison. Just a civil wedding of course. Our church one, our real one, will only take place when you're free. In fact, even a church wedding won't be quite complete for us, will it, without Michael. I'm afraid there's terrible news about Michael but I'm getting muddled up now, so let's come back to us first.

Stefan didn't need to turn over the page to read the bad news. He had read this letter so often in odd precious moments during the last few days.

It's your Gethsemane, Michael, he thought; and again he prayed that today of all days there might be a ray of Easter hope for his friend in the harsh regime labour camp connected to coalmines in the remote Tarlovian region.

Stefan's thoughts drifted back from Michael to Martha's proposal.

I know it's supposed to be the man who proposes, but you see, getting married is the only way I'll ever be able to visit you. Besides, it's hard for your mother to get time off work. Well, you know how difficult it is. I mean, she doesn't like to tell her supervisor the reason. In fact she's wondering if she'll be able to get away next time. Stefan, I can't bear the thought of you being without a visit. So what do you think, my dear, special Stefan? I know we haven't even had an official engagement, but we're not very official people, are we? Think it over and tell me what you decide.

Stefan shifted on the bunk, choking as the air became heavy with tobacoo smoke. He coughed as Milos, the black marketeer, blew smoke rings in his direction.

'Hot water in shower room B!' The news was spreading round the hut. Stefan folded Martha's letter, snatched up a sliver of coarse soap, a thin towel and joined the crush outside the showers. An hour later he

13

caught the last trickle of tepid water and tried to bring some sort of cleanliness to himself and his clothes.

Marry Martha now . . . but the marriage would just be on paper. True enough a visit would ease the long months of prison, but with eight months left to serve, Stefan could only expect two more meetings with his next of kin; and even that was entirely dependent on the authorities, who could cancel the visit at a moment's notice on any pretext whatsoever.

Marry Martha now? He wrung out the problem with his shirt. It would give Martha a new name, Mrs Cornelius. Oh, Martha, Martha, do you really want to be the wife of a convict? I love you so much, and I wish it was me and not baby Niki you were holding close like that!

'Get a move on, Cornelius,' urged the mathematician who was next in line.

'Sorry, Doctor,' Stefan apologised. 'How's the algebra coming on?'

'The complex case is as complex as ever – like friction applied to laundry without soap,' Doctor Volski replied, rubbing a torn sock.

'I'll work that one out later, Professor,' Stefan returned, 'but it looks like the hole in your sock is getting bigger every minute.'

'As large and as empty as life,' the mathematician sighed, grabbing the scrap of towel around his waist which kept threatening to come adrift. 'Now there's a riddle which matches the complexities of mathematics, my dear young Stefan.'

'I expect you're right,' agreed Stefan, out of his depth already.

My life may not be large, but it isn't empty, even in prison, he thought, and as his only set of clothes dried in the smoke-filled atmosphere, he wrote back to Martha.

Martha, my one and only love and the best girl in all the world.

The censor would drool, but most of the men here conducted some sort of love affair by letter.

Easter Greetings to you, and of course, pass them on to

Helen, Nikolai and my mother. Christ has risen and I wish I could put into words how happy I feel even though I'm in prison, even though I was too late in line to get any hot water, as usual, even though you're so far away from me. Do you know what I'm trying to say? Although things are difficult, we're definitely not left to face them on our own.

Least of all me, as I read in your letter. Dearest Martha, your proposal makes me very happy, but I don't want us to get married yet, not because I don't want to see you. I do, of course I do. I kiss your photographs all the time, and your letters. There, can you feel a special kiss just for you?

But just the same, I think we should wait. It's going to put you to too much hassle, and it will all be noted down too. For the rest of your life your marriage certificate will say: husband in prison. Don't you see, it's as bad as a police record for you too. I know you'll say you don't mind. Your love and generosity are too much for me. I simply don't deserve them, but time here is passing and God will give us strength to endure.

May he give that strength to our friend too, and to my brother, George. I notice you say in his letter that his engagement has broken off.

He turned back to Martha's letter.

The news about George isn't so good either. He's drinking a lot. Your mother is very worried about him, and I feel so bad, because she's got enough troubles to cope with.

Yes, Stefan reflected. Mother hasn't had it easy, either. She's not a Party person, and she didn't like it when George conformed to the regime, but at least she had the security of knowing that everything was rosy for him. Not now, it seems.

Tell Mother I'm sad to hear about George, Stefan wrote. *I'm sad about our other friend too. What terrible news! Yet I believe that God has given him a special blessing today in spite of everything.*

He stared into space and for a moment the over-crowded smoky hut faded from his awareness. He sensed the presence of his friend, Michael, thin and ill, his grey hair shorn as it had been when Stefan first met him in a punishment cell on the eve of Easter. Stefan had been a teenage soldier with all his thoughts set on promotion, but now . . . Well, we're alike in being bald, he thought ruefully, and ran his fingers across his shorn head. Regular detention in punishment cells deprived Stefan and Andrey even of the close crop allowed labourers in the supposedly light regime of the building site.

'Dinner time! Line up!' ordered their 'bosses', prisoners whose sentences had been reduced in return for keeping the others in check. They lined up outside the hut. Snow-capped peaks shone in April sunlight. The air was bitter. Everyone froze during the long wait for watery soup which bloated their insides but didn't fill them. Today being Sunday there was meat: rotten and tough, but hunger was stronger than squeamishness and there were no left-overs.

Stefan noticed Andrey ahead of him in the line. Contact with prisoners outside your own hut was forbidden, unless you happened to be put in the same work squad, but when he emerged, still hungry, from the prisoners' canteen, Andrey detached himself from a queue outside a latrine and followed Stefan's zigzag path across frozen rubble towards the clump of scrubby pine trees where they had met that morning.

'I saw you were taking a roundabout route, so I guessed you were heading here,' he said. 'I've made something for you. Happy Easter, Stefan.'

'For me? Andrey, what's this?'

'It's an ichthus fish,' he explained. 'I decided to make it after they beat you up for wearing a cross. It's only a few nails twisted together, so it wasn't hard to make. It's always been a secret sign, you know.'

'But why a fish?' wondered Stefan.

'Ichthus is Greek for fish, but it also stands for the first letters of the Greek words Iesus Christos, and the "*thus*" part at the end means Theou Huois – Son of God,' Andrey explained. 'The "s" stands for Soter, Saviour.'

'Jesus Christ, Son of God, Saviour,' Stefan repeated. 'Ichthus. I really appreciate that. Thanks very much,

Andrey.'

'That's all right, but is anything wrong? Something's worrying you today, Stefan, isn't it?'

'I've had bad news about Michael Laski. He's not allowed visits or parcels. His wife, Helen, travels miles and miles to see him, but they never let her near him. She's sure that the kilogram parcel she goes all that way to give him doesn't reach him either. He was concussed after one beating, but instead of giving him any treatment they beat him up again.'

'That's grim,' Andrey agreed. 'Did you have a letter?'

'Yes, from Martha. I think she got the news from Thomas Niski. Do you remember me telling you about Thomas, the electrician in Tarnov who was involved in the printing outfit they got me for?'

'The guy you said always likes to be where the action is . . .'

'Did I say that? It sounds a bit critical. I'm sorry. Thomas has always been kind to me.'

Though he was miffed when I took Martha out instead of his sister Elizabeth, he thought, remembering the time there had almost been a rift between himself and Thomas, and recalling Thomas's prickly feelings about Martha.

I did worse things than Martha ever has, yet it seems like Thomas can forgive me and not her, he thought; but aloud he said, 'Thomas promised Michael he'd look after Helen and Nikolai. From what Martha tells me, he certainly tries to stay in touch. Like just now, over this latest news. The feeling we all have is that they're trying to kill Michael, just like they did when he was inside last time. In fact they've told him openly that they won't let him out alive.'

They stared at the ground in silence.

A couple of underfed crows landed on the patch of frozen snow at their feet, pecked around and flew off again.

'Even crows go hungry here,' Andrey said.

Stefan nodded, but he was trying to work out a plan

he wanted to share with Andrey. 'You know I was sent to work here for nine months when I was fifteen?* That was five years, ago, he added. 'I met Michael's long-lost friend . . .'

'Brother Nikolai,' Andrey recalled. 'That book of his prison letters you and your friends printed has fired so many people all over Koravia, and abroad too, it seems. So, take heart, Stefan. It cost you your freedom, I know, but the effect on a whole lot of us who were secret Christians was explosive. After all, some of us students were the very ones the regime tried hardest to win over. But once we read those letters we knew we mustn't hold back any more; that's the way my friend Leo puts it. We had to nail our faith on the line like Nikolai . . . I could hardly believe it when you told me you'd actually met him here in this prison camp.'

'I always called him Nik,' Stefan said. 'He was my friend. He gave me an orange – I've never forgotten how good it tasted! He went on hunger strike for me, even though he had cancer. I got hospital treatment, but Nik got sent to the coalmines where he died. And now they've put Michael there. It's perfectly true what they say: they're not likely to let him out alive. But, listen, Andrey, I know what I've got to do now. If Nik could do all that for me, I can do it for Michael.

'Do what? Go on hunger strike, you mean? They'll punish you for that . . .' Andrey began.

'But at least they'll know that we know about Michael, and if we know, shut away here, it's going to be obvious other people will know too, people in Koravia and further away. Public opinion is beginning to count for something in Koravia at last. Pray for me, Andrey.'

* This story is told in Dark Journey.

2

Sold with silence

'Rrrrrr! Rrrrrrr!' Niki toddled up to the bed settee where Martha was curled up, writing a letter to Stefan.

'Rrrrrr!' repeated Martha, busy writing.

> *Lipa,*
> *Friday, 10th November.*
> *Four weeks and two days before THE DAY THEY SET YOU FREE! I can't wait. Oh, Stefan, do you know it's four months since your last letter? But I'm not going to think about that. I'm just going to think about you coming home. We'll spend Christmas together . . .*

'What is it then, Niki?' She picked him up. 'Oh, you've brought me a tiger picture. Arrrgh!' she roared, eating Niki up. His chuckles brought his mother, Helen, into Martha's room.

'Caught you, Niki! We were trying to give you a peaceful moment, Martha, on your day off.'

'It doesn't matter. I was just writing to Stefan. Our last letter before he's released! I can't wait to have him home, but it's worrying me that I haven't heard from him for so long . . .' Martha checked herself, not wanting to say too much. It was two years since Helen had heard from her husband.

'I'm sure Stefan's written. They must be holding up his letters. It will be part of their punishment for all his hunger strikes . . . three since Easter. He's going through all this because he cares so much for Michael.'

'Rrrrrr!' insisted Niki. Martha hugged him to her. 'You're a little tiger, Niki, and I could eat you up. Do you know who's coming all the way from Kostka to see us? Joanna is.'

'–ana nis,' repeated Niki.

'Jo–anna,' corrected his mother, and Martha knew that Helen's thoughts had gone to thirteen year old Joanna's father, Adam Puls, the ploughman who had been locked away from his family for the last three years because he had tried to re–open the church in his village, Kostka, which the authorities had closed. Michael and Helen had continued to help the people of Kostka hold services outside the closed church, and more and more people had attended them, until Michael had been arrested in his turn, together with Stefan.*

But Niki had spotted Martha's pen. 'Mmm . . .' he began, holding out his hand.

'No, Niki, you'll get ink all over you. Remember how he painted his hands when we were making harvest cards?'

'I certainly do! Listen, there's someone at the door. It will probably be Joanna.'

But when they opened the door the tall, crisp figure of Stefan's friend, Thomas Niski, greeted them.

'Come in, Thomas,' Helen invited him. 'How are your mother and sister?'

'They're fine, thank you. Elizabeth has got a place in the Students' Orchestra. There's even a chance she'll play with the Tarnov Philharmonic next summer.'

'That's very good. It's only her second year at music school, isn't it? She must be progressing well in her flute playing.'

'Oh, she is, but listen, there's news,' Thomas added as they sat him down at the kitchen table and poured out tea.

'A campaign for Michael,' he said in a low voice.

'Not here in Koravia?' Helen asked.

'Abroad as well. Human rights groups in totalitarian and open countries have made his case a priority. Especially in Ostrova, that's the country abroad that Dr

* *Their story is told in Light Sentence.*

Green, that woman you met, comes from, Martha. Their Foreign Secretary is visiting Koravia in the New Year. She – the Foreign Secretary I mean, is going to make representations to our government on Michael's behalf.'

'Thank God! Oh, let her be successful!'

'Yes. Our Party Secretary really seems to be listening to what governments outside our set-up are saying about human rights here. But you know, the action in Koravia is all because of Stefan's hunger strikes. Brother Leo is organising a petition.'

'Who's he?' asked Martha.

'He works in Holy Cross Church; you know, the one in Tarnov Old Town. He's a good guy. He's already done time. It seems he knows Andrey, that friend Stefan writes about. Leo says the time has come for open action. No more silent collaboration.'

'That's amazing,' said Helen. 'No, Niki, careful, it's hot.' She pushed the tea things out of Niki's reach and set the toddler on the ground. Martha gave him a box to play with.

'I know; it's so different from the mealy-mouthed stuff the "official" clergy spew out from the pulpit,' Thomas went on. 'Leo's very outspoken. Last week he said publicly that a few silver pieces were enough for the most righteous man who ever lived to be sold to corrupt organs of government. The whole atmosphere was electric.'

'Those were brave words,' Helen agreed.

'Yes, but wait till you hear this . . .' Thomas went on enthusiastically.

Thomas means well, Martha thought to herself, but he's a bit too sure of himself. He's always the one in the know.

She bent towards Niki and gave him a wooden spoon to put in and out of his box, but Thomas's next words riveted her attention back to him.

'Leo actually mentioned Michael and Stefan.'

'In his sermon?' asked Helen.

'What did he say?' demanded Martha.

'Everyone's talking about it,' said Thomas. 'Leo said

that two years ago the leaders of our church sold not with silver, but with silence a man who was known as a light for Koravia.'

'I can't believe this!' Helen put her face in her hands. 'Dear God, is there some hope then, after all?'

'He meant Michael, of course!' said Martha. 'Oh, Thomas, that's tremendous news! But you said it was all because of Stefan's hunger strikes? Do you know I haven't had a single letter for four months?'

'Yes, Leo knows about that too. Andrey managed to smuggle out all the info. Leo said as much.'

'You mean, this Leo guy said all that in his sermon?' asked Martha.

'Not in his sermon, no, but he prayed for Michael and Stefan by name. I'm telling you,' Thomas added, raising his voice as Niki started to clatter saucepan lids together, 'there won't be a single empty space in that church next Sunday.'

'I expect you're right. No, Niki,' Helen removed the offending lids. 'Oh, you're wet through.'

'I wonder where Joanna can be?' Martha said. 'She's much later than she said she'd be. I'll go and change Niki, shall I, Helen?'

'Oh, yes, please. Will you stay and have supper with us, Thomas? I'm making potato fritters and we've got some pickled cabbage. All home grown. There's no meat, but perhaps you're keeping the Advent fast like us?'

'Trying to,' Thomas said, 'but if there is any meat available, you may be sure my mother will stand in a queue to buy it. She says our diet is so poor most of the year we can't afford to fast.'

'I suppose she's got a point,' Helen said. 'I must admit I put as much protein as I can into Martha's meals. She's going through enough as it is, as well as working long shifts in the factory. So you'll stay, then?'

'Yes, please, if it's not too much trouble for you.'

'Not at all. Oh, listen, there is Joanna now. It's high time I got the potatoes on.'

'Is there anything I can help you with?'

'Yes, open the door for Joanna, if you would, Thomas.'

Joanna Puls was already taking off her coat. As Niki solemnly held out a pair of slippers for her, Thomas asked Martha, 'How does Helen keep so cheerful?'

'She's had years of practice,' Martha pointed out. 'Of course, Niki's a help, but if you want an answer, Thomas, I don't know. I mean, I've got Stefan's release to look forward to. Though I must say it's worrying not getting any letters . . . How was school today, Joanna?'

'All right. I got an A for cookery, but I've got better news than that,' Joanna said.

Martha put Niki into a chair at the table. 'Tell us all about it then, Joanna.'

'It's Dad,' Joanna said.

'What? What? Tell us.'

'He's going to be moved.'

'Moved? Where to? How do you know?'

'Mum had a visit from the police. They were there when I came home from school. They weren't wearing uniform, but I could tell at once who they were.'

'What did they say?' Helen asked.

'I was scared,' Joanna began, 'but they weren't rough or anything. Mum made them tea and they sat and talked. They said that Dad will be moved to a different sort of hospital . . .'

'He doesn't need to be in hospital at all,' Martha interrupted.

'Mum told them that as well,' explained Joanna.

'Right to their faces?' queried Thomas. 'Good for her! She's very brave.'

'She's had to be,' Martha couldn't help reminding him. 'From the day the police dragged Adam away and pumped injections into him. Anyway, let Joanna get on with her story. Did they say what sort of hospital it would be?'

Joanna wrinkled her face, trying to remember. 'A sana, sana-something.'

'Sanatorium,' Helen supplied the word.

'That's it. He won't be locked up when he's there. He'll be able to walk about outside, they said, and they're going to stop giving him injections too.'

'Oh, that *is* good news! But when will it happen?' asked Helen.

'They didn't say. Soon.'

'What's all this about a sanatorium, though?' asked Martha, mashing egg up for Niki. 'Why can't they send him straight home?'

'Adam's been locked up in that Psychiatric Prison for almost three years. He'll probably need a bit of time to adjust to being in a more open atmosphere without any drugs and injections,' Thomas pointed out, and Helen agreed, but Martha wasn't convinced.

'However open it is, that sanatorium is still controlled by *them*,' she said, spooning egg into Niki's mouth. 'Your dad won't be happy until he's home, Joanna, and nor will we, but of course it's great news just the same. Now, all we need is a letter from Stefan and news that Michael is going to be allowed to receive treatment. They keep saying things are easing up in our country, but I won't believe that until we have Stefan and Michael home.'

'I know how you feel, Martha,' Helen began, and Thomas cut in, 'Here's another piece of news for you. There's talk of a Christmas Eve service being televised from Tarnov Cathedral.'

'Big deal! I'd rather have Stefan home!'

'No, but it's the first time such a thing will have happened in our country,' Helen said, 'so it is an important event. I'm going to dish up our dinner now.'

Martha lifted Niki down and washed the remains of his dinner from his hands and face. They stood around the table.

'As we thank our Lord for our food and for the good news that we've heard, we pray for those we love,' Helen said. As she finished her prayer, the door opened. Stefan's mother, Maria, came in. Helen went over to help

Maria hang up her winter coat. 'How was work? Busy, I suppose, as usual at this time of year,' she began, but the look on her friend's face made Helen check herself. 'Is anything wrong?' she asked, dropping her voice.

Maria nodded. 'It's Stefan,' she began.

'What is it?' Martha burst out. 'He's all right, isn't he?'

'Oh, yes, dear. At least, they didn't say there's anything wrong. There's been a letter from prison.'

'A letter? From Stefan?'

'No, from the authorities. I found it when I got home from work.'

'What is it? What did it say? Oh, Maria, it's bad news, isn't it?'

'Steady, Martha,' Thomas cautioned.

'Stefan won't be home for Christmas,' his mother looked at the letter she was holding.

'But he's due for release in four weeks,' Martha protested.

'December 10th, isn't it?' Thomas put in. 'That's exactly two years since he was sentenced. What's gone wrong, Mrs Cornelius? Why aren't they letting him out?'

'They've extended his sentence,' Maria began. 'No, Martha, dear, don't look like that; don't cry. The main thing is that Stefan's all right.'

'But we were looking forward to having him home for Christmas!'

'I know. It's kept us all going, hasn't it?' Helen said. Her arm was round Martha's shoulders. 'Does the letter say when Stefan is likely to be released now?'

'They say it should be March 10th – another three months . . .

'Three months! That's not till spring! He's got the whole winter ahead of him; all the worst of the cold is still to come.'

'I know, Martha, I know,'

'So much for all that talk about openness!' Thomas commented. 'Do they give any reasons, Mrs Cornelius?'

'An infringement of regulations, that's all.'

'That means nothing at all,' said Thomas.

'It means what they want it to mean,' Helen said. 'But to us it means victory.'

'Victory? What do you mean, Helen?'

'It means that Stefan has been pressing them hard. It's their way of retaliating. It's stupid and vindictive, but it's a sign that he's challenging them all the way along the line,' Helen said firmly. 'We've got to hold on to that, Martha. He knew what the consequences of his hunger strikes would be. Force feeding, yes, and punishment as well. He did it for Michael. He's a fighter, and we must support him every way we can.'

'Yes, Helen, you're right. Besides,' Martha gulped, catching back a sob, 'you know better than me what it means to be without the man you love.' She broke free from Helen's comforting arm and filled the kettle. 'I'm sure you need a cup of tea, Maria. Helen's got your dinner ready for you.'

'Yes, what a treat! I've brought us a jar of honey. A woman from work brought it from her own hives. Stefan always liked her honey.'

'Honey! That's the very thing for Stefan's Christmas parcel!' exclaimed Helen. 'Can you get another jar, do you think, Maria?'

'I'll try. Yes, of course, we'll have to get that parcel ready soon.'

'I've been knitting for him,' Joanna said.

'She's very good,' Martha added. 'Not like me. I drop all the stitches. Did you know Joanna got good marks for her cookery? We'll have to make a nice parcel up for your dad as well, Joanna,' Martha went on. 'Oh, but, they will allow Stefan to have a Christmas parcel, won't they?'

'We must hope so,' Maria tried to reassure her, and Helen added, 'Surely,' as she made the tea. But they all knew that her husband received no parcels and that even the Christmas card she sent him would be confiscated by the guards.

Thomas broke a sad silence. 'We must pull out all the

stops to make the campaign for Michael successful,' he said. 'After all, look what's happening to Adam.'

'We haven't told you yet, Maria,' Martha put in, cuddling Niki. 'Joanna's good news wasn't only about cookery.'

'The police told us today that Dad's to be moved to a – what was it, Helen?'

'A sanatorium,' Thomas supplied. 'Things will be more open for him, and it looks like the first step towards him getting home.'

'Away from that terrible hospital at last!' exclaimed Maria. 'How relieved your mother must feel! Will you be able to visit your dad, Joanna?'

'Yes, the police said we could, but I'm not really sure I'll recognise him,' Joanna nodded. 'I mean, there are photographs at home, but they were mostly taken a long time ago. I was only ten when they arrested him.'

'He'll see a big change in you, Joanna,' Helen said, and talk stayed firmly around the Puls family's hopes to get their father home, until Niki started rubbing his eyes.

'Can I put him to bed, Helen?' Martha asked.

'Of course. He loves it when you tuck him up!'

'I'd better get back to Tarnov. There's a train in ten minutes, I think.' Thomas stood up. 'Thanks for the meal.'

'Thank you for coming with your news,' Helen replied. 'We appreciate the way you keep in touch with us.'

'I wish I could do more. I'll tell Brother Leo this latest news,' Thomas said, shaking hands.

'Say "night-night", Niki,' instructed Martha, and Niki obediently echoed her words and waved Thomas goodbye.

'Night-night, Niki,' Thomas replied, but to everyone's surprise he bent down and gave Martha an awkward kiss. 'You're very brave. Stefan will be proud of you.'

His unexpected praise was too much for Martha. She put Niki down and raced out of the room.

'What have I done wrong?' Thomas asked, 'I only tried to encourage her.'

'And so you did, Thomas,' Helen reassured him, and Maria added, 'Martha needed to have a good cry all on her own. But you must get away for your train, Thomas, and we must get everything together for Stefan's Christmas parcel.'

'Send him my best wishes,' said Thomas, opening the door.

'Of course,' they agreed.

3

Target Fulfilled

'No!' the shout awoke Stefan. Who had shouted? He
stared into the darkness, sweating. Only moments ago
he had seen four men bend over him. 'No!' he had
screamed. 'No!'

In nightmares like these he relived torture. They'd
wrenched his mouth open and thrust tubes down his
throat. Boiling liquid seared his famished gut. Screams
gurgled in his throat, muffled by clamps and tubes.
Tears scalded his eyes. Afterwards, left alone, he'd
sobbed: hurt, animal cries, violated, debased,
minimized.

For Michael's sake, though, he refused to give up.

Awake now in early March dawn, Stefan came to
himself.

It was only a dream. It's over now. I've only got nine
days to go, but will they release me this time? They
must.

There was no 'must' about it, he knew. *They* had total
power here. All he had was the conviction that evil must
not win.

He had nothing else: and yet sometimes strength came
unasked. Weakened by hunger and punishment, cold,
unwell, he would feel a sudden sense of well-being. He
could go on then, comforted.

When it was all over, the hunger strikes and punishment cell, the confiscation of letters, cancellation of
visits, Stefan told Andrey about this comforting sense of
well-being.

'It seemed as if someone was with me, helping me.

It's not the first time I've felt like that,' Stefan went on. 'It happened sometimes when I was locked up before my trial. Michael was in prison then as well, but he didn't feel anything good at all, Andrey, and he's a much better person than me.'

'You've laid yourself open to torture for the sake of your friend,' Andrey said. 'They promised their government would bring us a revolution when everyone will share a good life, but all we see is people exploiting one another. You are resisting evil, and that's why you get given extra strength.'

'But I go under so easily,' Stefan objected. 'These nightmares . . .'

'No wonder, after the horrors they put you through. The whole of Koravia knows about it.'

'The main thing is that they know about Michael. He'll die if they don't set him free. Things are supposed to be getting freer in Koravia – but not for Michael Laski.'

All the same, changes were afoot. Three weeks before Easter, and a whole week before Stefan's release was due, they let him go free.

A guard came into the hut very early in the morning and shook Stefan awake.

'Superintendent wants to see you. Get a move on.' He urged Stefan outside into the darkness.

'What is it this time?'

'Another six months, most likely.'

The guard was wrong. They signed his release and told him to go.

Prison gates clanged behind him.

Andrey wasn't even up.

They gave him a ticket for the train, but nothing else, no money, no warm clothing. At least he had Martha's photographs and Andrey's ichthus fish. These treasures had survived searches and strippings, and now, during the slow journey to Tarnov, Stefan looked at them often.

There was no one to meet him, but he had found a small coin under one of the wooden benches on the train and phoned Thomas Niski's home.

'Stefan! Don't you know, there was going to be an enormous welcome for you. Listen, when's your next train home to Lipa?'

'Not for two hours.'

Two hours and then the journey home. Another five hours before he saw Martha!

'That's fifteen ten. Okay, I'll come across right now and meet you.'

'I'm glad I was at home when you rang,' Thomas said when he met Stefan. 'I'm on a late shift today. They did this deliberately, you know.'

'Did what?' Stefan's thoughts never kept pace with Thomas. Besides, he was still half in the labour camp, and he hadn't had anything to eat or drink all day.

'Sent you home before schedule, so that no one would be able to give you a big public welcome. I mean, you're famous, Stefan. But listen, Dr. Green, that woman from Ostrova, has friends who visit Koravia. They left this for you.'

He handed Stefan a bulging plastic bag with foreign trademarks. 'Shows the way things are changing here. Not long ago we'd never have dared be seen carrying bags with trademarks from countries outside our system.'

'What's inside?'

'All sorts of things. Vitamin pills for a start, and ant-acids to help your stomach pains. How are you feeling, by the way?'

'Not bad.'

'I made you a sandwich in case you haven't eaten. Here you are. I'll go and buy you a drink. Cold juice or tea?'

'Whichever's easiest. Thanks, Thomas. I haven't any money, though.'

'As if that matters!'

Stefan sat on a seat and unwrapped a piece of bread smeared with pickled tomato, but he found he could eat very little.

'I guess I'm keyed up at the thought of coming home,' he told Thomas. Of seeing Martha, he thought. We've been apart so long, and now that there's hardly any time to wait, I can't last out.

What would she look like? The last photograph had been taken months ago. She'd written that she was growing her hair.

He shut his eyes for a moment, picturing Martha, and then tried to pull himself together and concentrate on Thomas's news.

'Michael's name was mentioned on the foreign news last night. After the Ostrovan Foreign Secretary's visit here the Party actually agreed to take part in an international conference on human rights. We're pinning our hopes on that, Stefan. Helen still hears nothing from Michael. She's gone very grey.

No, not grey, white. Stefan stared in amazement as Helen opened her back door. She looked strained and ill, but her face lit up with a smile.

'Stefan! Home at last. How wonderful! Won't Martha be pleased! She's still at work. But come in, come in,' she went on, leading him into the kitchen, where a curly-haired toddler was busily lining up teapots and plastic toys.

'That can't be Niki!'

'Oh, Stefan, it is. Martha wanted to be the one to show him off to you. We've sewn him a new little suit specially, and look at him now in his old clothes. Niki, look who's come home!'

'Hello, Niki,' Stefan said, a little awkwardly.

The unfamiliar voice caught Niki's attention. He turned round, and Stefan's mind was caught in a time warp. Michael's steady eyes looked up at him from his son's small face.

'It's Stefan,' Helen was saying.

Stefan lowered himself to Niki's level. 'You're busy here, aren't you?' he said.

Niki held out a teapot lid. 'I cooking,' he announced.

'He's just learning to talk,' Helen said. 'But I'm sure you're hungry, Stefan. I've got some soup here for our supper. Let me see, what's the time? Goodness, it's quarter to seven. Your mother won't be home until around eight tonight.' Helen ladled the soup into bowls and lifted Niki on to his chair. 'It's not much of a welcome feast, I'm afraid.'

'Oh, but it is,' he assured her, 'only I wish it were Michael and not just me.'

'Soup, soup,' clamoured Niki.

Helen guided his spoon. She glanced up at Stefan. Her eyes beneath the crown of white hair were very solemn. 'Stefan, my dear, I can never thank you enough for what you've done for Michael!'

He shook his head. 'It was the only thing to do.'

Niki's spoon splattered into his soup. 'Now, Niki,' scolded Helen. 'What would Martha say? She's wonderful, Stefan,' she went on, 'I don't know what I would do without her. I want to pay for a taxi for you to meet her from work. You can both ride home in style. No, Stefan, take it,' she insisted, as he tried to refuse money he knew Helen couldn't afford. 'You don't want to hang around waiting for buses tonight. Would you like more soup?'

'No thanks, Helen. I'd like to get home and have a wash before I meet Martha.'

'Oh, Stefan, what am I thinking of! Martha and I made you a shirt. Your mother bought some new things for you too, just whenever anything nice happened to come into the shops . . . Wait a minute. I'll fetch the shirt. Here you are. Now, are you sure you won't have anything more to eat?'

No, he wouldn't, and he hoped Helen wouldn't think he was ungracious, but he wanted to get home. He unlocked the kitchen door and looked about him. Home again, in the house of his childhood. The kitchen was warm. Everything was just as he remembered it. He went to the sink and turned on the tap. After a few moments the water came hot. He stripped off his prison clothes and stood there naked, soaping, lathering, shaving, enjoying the luxury of hot water, privacy and a soft clean towel. He wrapped it round him and went into the living room where his couch was covered with its usual day-time cover. He ran his fingers across his stubbly head. Oh, Martha, Martha, you'll see a shorn scarecrow when you come through the factory gates tonight, stick-thin and scalped. What will all your friends think?

Still, the new shirt was nice, just the thing he and Martha liked with its traditional Koravian embroidery. Her fingers had sewn those stitches for him, and he kissed the shirt before he put it on.

He found a pair of trousers. Too wide in the waist, and he had never been fat. He had to make another hole in the belt he pulled around him. Hanging behind the door was his father's peasant style hat. Martha liked him in it. He would wear it at nine o'clock when he went to meet her. Meantime he propped her photographs on the sideboard beside the old ones of him and his brother George. Time must surely be creeping on, but there was still something left to do – Andrey's ichthus fish. He had taken it out of his pocket when he'd stripped off his clothes. He went back into the kitchen for it. He let it lie on his open palm: nails and wire twisted together for an Easter gift almost a year ago. Would Andrey realise that Stefan had been released?

Alone in the warm kitchen Stefan prayed for Andrey, still with time to serve, and for Michael. Then he nailed Andrey's Easter gift beside the wooden cross which had hung above the tiled stove for as long as he could remember and as he did so, the door opened and his mother came in, burdened with shopping as usual, wearing the same winter coat she always wore.

Stefan moved forward to hug her.

'Hello, Mother . . .'

'Stefan! Is it really you? After so long! How are you? Oh, why didn't they let us know you were coming? Let me have a look at you. Oh, my goodness . . .' There were tears in her eyes. Was she remembering that first homecoming of his from prison when he was only a teenager and had been sentenced for pulling down a Party flag . . . Poor Mother. I've put you through so much.

It had never been their way to make a fuss about things. Maria blinked back her tears, freed him from her embrace and said briskly, 'Does Martha know you've come home?'

'Not yet. I'm going to meet her.'

Talk filled the quiet kitchen.

'There's hardly any food – I wasn't expecting you.'

'It's all right . . . I can't eat much.'

'I'll just look in that bag. There's some caraway bread.'

'Don't you cook for yourself then?'

'Not often. I eat in the works canteen. Sometimes Helen and I share meals. How thin you are! Mind you, George is looking dreadful. I was in Tarnov last week and I bumped into him. Oh, Stefan, I shouldn't be telling you all this when you're hardly in the door.'

'I've been in for about half an hour,' Stefan reminded his mother. 'I should have put the kettle on for you. I'm sorry.'

'You can't be expected to think of everything. Half an hour did you say?'

'I had a wash and changed.' He bundled up his prison clothes. 'There's only one place for these – the bin.'

'Yes, of course. Now, where's the knife?'

'I'll cut that bread. So you've seen George?'

'Yes, hungover. You know things are changing in Koravia?'

'So everyone keeps saying,' Stefan said through a mouthful of fresh bread.

'It's good bread, isn't it? Have some more. Here's some salad. How about cheeses?'

'No, that's all right. Helen gave me soup. So, what's new? Not much if everyone's hungover.'

'Not everyone . . . George has made enemies, it seems.'

'That's nothing new either. Oh, I'm sorry, Mother. I

didn't mean to sound sarcastic. Enemies, you said. In the army, you mean?'

'Yes. Heads are beginning to roll, and George is highly enough placed to be at risk. His drinking doesn't help, either, but what about yourself? You've been into Helen's, then? Did she give you our key?'

'That's how I got in. She gave me money too, to get a taxi when I meet Martha.'

'How kind of her! You'd better go out and phone for one at once. What a surprise it will be for Martha! You look nice in that shirt, but we'll have to fatten you up a bit. Will you be able to stay here or do you have to go to Tarnov?'

'I'll have to register with the police. I suppose they'll tell me what I'm allowed to do.'

'Things will sort themselves out,' Maria assured him. 'The main thing is that you've come home.'

'Do you really mean that? I've brought you nothing but trouble.' He hesitated. 'Did George say anything about me, Mother?'

'He wasn't in a fit state to say much about anybody,' Maria replied.

'I'd like to meet him again,' Stefan said.

Maria Cornelius looked enquiringly at her younger son. 'Would you, Stefan? You haven't always been the best of friends.'

'I know.'

Did his mother know that George had organised Stefan's last arrest?

He beat me to the ground, but he's beaten now, Stefan thought. George was just their instrument. I would have been arrested anyway.

He wasn't sure what Martha would think about too much contact with his brother . . .

We'll just have to see, he thought, and aloud he said, 'I'll go and phone for a taxi. Do you have a coin, Mother?'

'Yes, of course. Here you are. Oh, you've found your father's hat. I must say it suits you.'

'Better than the scalped look. I'm a bit embarrassed at meeting Martha with my head like a baboon's backside.'

'Stefan, my dear, she's been eating her heart out for you. Your hair will soon grow.'

It took Stefan some time to find a phone box but at last he made his call and set off home along slushy pavements. Sleepy Lipa streets dozed in dim light. Several roofs now sprouted television aerials, and garden paths were occupied by small square Koravian cars.

It was a locally made car known as a 'Koravia' which bounced Stefan along the rutted highway out of Lipa towards the factory where Martha worked.

'Going on night shift, are you?'

'No, meeting a friend. Can you take us back again?'

'Sure. Did you watch the football the other night?'

'Um, no . . . was it a good game?'

'A good game? We won the European cup! Where have you been these last few days?'

'Away.'

'Ah, a ski-ing holiday then?'

'No, work.'

'Ah!' the driver said meaningfully, and asked no more questions but Stefan guessed he'd be wondering what his scrawny looking passenger did for a living, that took him away from important football games, and allowed him to ride in a taxi to a factory simply to 'meet a friend'.

They pulled up outside a building which proclaimed: Honour our workers who fulfil their targets!

'Can you wait here?' Stefan asked.

'Okay.' The driver switched off his engine and struck a match. In its light Stefan saw a small medallion swinging from the dashboard. Stefan opened the door. The courtesy light came on and he could see a lamb with a halo etched on the medallion.

Honour our workers who fulfil their targets, declared the regime, but the symbol of the Lamb of God hanging in that Koravian taxi bore silent witness to its driver's different sympathies.

Neon–lit workers hurried home in twos and threes.

Stefan stood beside the gate, waiting.

Supposing Martha comes through those gates with her arms round someone else? No, no, how could he think like that? Oh, Martha, I've missed you so much! I can't think straight any more.

Oh, here she is. She's tired, I can see. She was crying and waving when I last saw her, and throwing flowers. That was in Tarnov Court, the day of my trial, and Michael's, more than two years ago. I haven't got any flowers for her, nothing.

'Martha . . . dearest Martha!'

'Stefan? Oh, it can't be true. Stefan!'

Her arms were round him now.

'Martha, oh, Martha!'

And there was nothing to say, but only kiss . . . and then there was everything to say . . .

'Where are you going? The bus stop's over there!'

'Not for us. There's a taxi waiting for us tonight.'

'A taxi? Have you become a black marketeer?'

'Helen paid. She wanted to give us both a treat. Yes, please, back to Lipa. Martha, Martha, let me look at you.'

'I made myself a new dress specially for you coming home, and here I am in a factory overall . . . You're wearing your new shirt.'

'Made by you . . .'

'And Helen. So she knows you're home. Was Niki still up? What did he say?'

'Not much. Oh, Martha, I've waited so long for this!'

'I've waited too.'

'I know . . . You said you were growing your hair, but it's covered with your scarf.'

'I have to keep it like that for work.' Martha pulled off her scarf and shook her hair loose. 'It's getting long, see.'

'Let me feel.' He ran his fingers through Martha's dark curls.

'I'll lend you some,' she offered. 'Poor Stefan! Still, it will grow.'

'Not soon enough. I didn't want you to see it scalped like this so soon, but of course I had to take my hat off in the presence of a lady.'

'What a gentleman! I appreciate that, too. I saw you were wearing it. In fact, I recognized the hat first and then you . . . oh, Stefan I could hardly believe it! Is it all a dream, do you think?'

'A sweet dream,' he told her, clasping his hand around hers.

'When did you know?'

'That I was coming home? This morning. What's the time?'

'I don't know. I haven't got a watch. Something after nine.'

'Well, it was something after four,' Stefan said. 'Seventeen hours ago. Every single minute seemed a lifetime. All I could think of was seeing you. This whole day has lasted longer than the last twenty–seven months put together, but now I don't want it to finish. Only I know I'll have to let you get home to bed. You'll need something to eat as well.'

Martha yawned. 'No, I'm not hungry. Only a bit tired.'

'Back at the same house, sir?'

'No, the house next door.'

'Not long ago he would have said "comrade",' Stefan commented after he'd paid the fare. 'Or was he making fun? Did he guess?'

'Guess what?'

'You know. Prison . . .'

'I shouldn't think so. Who cares if he did? You're not a criminal.'

'Just got a nice prison haircut.' He opened the gate. 'I couldn't kiss you in the taxi.'

So once again their lips spoke kisses, and it was a long time before they could bear to separate for the night.

4

Snowdrops for a bride

Sunshine filtered into Stefan's room. He yawned, and opened his eyes to find familiar furnishings around him.

Good to be back, to be free to sleep or get up, to eat – he was ravenously hungry, and know that the food would be fresh and wholesome. Free to see Martha!

He got up and pulled back the curtains. Children were playing in the school yard. Sunlight fretted birches and lime trees, still bare. Play-time always used to end at eleven o'clock, and, as though to remind him, the school bell rang.

He went through to the kitchen to fill the kettle. A scribbled message caught his attention.

I didn't want to waken you. Martha's still at home. Help yourself to food. I'll be home around five. Have a good rest.

Stefan rushed to get dressed. Shaving could wait, he decided. He hurried out into sunshine which was melting the last of the winter snow.

Martha called from the kitchen window: 'You're up at last! Come in, Stefan.'

They shared a good morning kiss. 'Nice smell of toothpaste,' Martha remarked.

'It was nice having some to use,' he returned. 'So you wouldn't mind another kiss?'

'Mmmm. Ow! Your chin's bristly.'

'Good morning, Helen. Hi, there, Niki! Any kisses for Uncle Stefan?'

'I want some too,' said Martha. 'From both of you,' she added in Stefan's ear as they hugged Niki and helped Helen set out bread and home-made jam.

'I still can't believe you're really home,' declared Martha, her mouth half full. 'I've been saving up my holidays for this.'

'I suppose you have got quite a lot of sorting out to do now, Stefan,' said Helen.

'I'll have to find out where I'm to be allowed to live for a start,' said Stefan.

'Nothing else?' quizzed Martha.

'I thought we might go over to Kostka and see the Puls family. Perhaps we could go and visit Adam too. Do you fancy that, Martha?'

'Yes . . .'

'You don't sound very certain.'

'Of course I'm certain, it's just I thought there might be something else you'd like to get organised as well. Not straight away, of course, but soon.'

'Oh?' he asked, and looked so puzzled that Martha had to laugh.

'Our wedding . . .' she began, and Stefan looked so surprised that Helen had to laugh too, but then Martha's smile faded.

'What is it?'

'Nothing. I just thought, that, well, you know: maybe you don't want to marry me after all.'

'Oh, Martha, Martha, of course I do!'

Wedding plans cropped up frequently during the next few days.

'I hope my hair's grown a bit,' Stefan said.

'More to the point, where do you think you're going to live?' his mother asked.

'I don't know. The police said I could still work in Tarnov Hospital, but not as a trainee nurse any more. I'll have to be a medical orderly.'

'Just what you were when we first met,' Martha reminded him as they swung Niki between them, walking across to Kostka. 'I'll never forget the way you filled up the water buckets for me and the other cleaners every morning. What a romantic beginning to our relationship!'

'Both of us working in a prison hospital! . . . Tell me what's been happening in Kostka while I've been away.'

'Not much. The authorities still won't register our church, but they gave Michael's old boss, Jan, his barn back, and so we hold our services there and the police don't seem to bother, but you never know, of course. Jan never misses a service either. I know it's all because of Michael. Oh, Stefan, how I wish we could hear from him! His name is mentioned on foreign news broadcasts, but Helen never gets a single letter.'

'It puts a cloud over our wedding, doesn't it? What is it, Niki?'

'He's getting tired.'

'Come up on my shoulders, then,' invited Stefan, and Martha helped him swing his godson into place.

'He's gorgeous, isn't he?'

'So are you . . .' he told her, and, on their way home, still carrying Niki on his shoulders, Stefan said, 'So you want to be Mrs Cornelius, then?'

'I guess so . . .'

'I haven't much to offer,' he began.

'I haven't much to give.'

'What do you mean? You've got everything! Knowing you loved me kept me going.'

'That's wonderful of you to say so . . . What about your friend Andrey? Hasn't he got a girl friend? He sounds so nice.'

'He is. He's very clever and studious, not at all the sort of person who would ever have anything to do with someone like me normally. Like we said, prison can be a good meeting place, and of course when people pray together all the usual barriers disappear at once. Andrey wants to enter seminary . . .'

'What does that mean?'

'You know, where people train to work in the church, but of course they'll never let someone like Andrey in. Andrey says if you're not an informer before you get in, the chances are very high you'll become one once you're there.'

But Stefan was still thinking over Martha's remark about not having much to give. It was only as they jolted on an ancient bus across winding countryside to visit Adam Puls in a ramshackle wooden building euphemistically called a sanatorium that Stefan said, 'Martha, you're not still thinking about your past, are you?'

'Why shouldn't I?' she flashed at him. 'You still think about yours. Oh, I'm sorry, Stefan, that's not right of me.'

'Yes, it is,' he told her. 'It's true. Everyone has their own past – and I did cruel, bad things.'

To Michael, of all people, he thought, though I tried to make up for it afterwards. Oh, let Michael have someone to care for him now!

'That isn't what I meant,' Martha was trying to explain. 'You got put into prison for vandalising a flag. That's not a crime. I know you got involved in rough things afterwards. But I . . . Oh, Stefan, I find it hard to talk about it, but I've got to know: does it really not worry you?'

'What?'

She hesitated and then as they got off the bus she said, 'That I'm not a virgin.'

'Martha, dear Martha, that's all in the past.'

'Will you think so on our wedding night?' she asked.

He took her hand. The path was muddy. Puddle water mirrored the sky.

'Spring is really on its way,' Martha said. 'Oh, look, Stefan, snowdrops!'

She bent over their nodding heads. 'Virgin white,' she said. 'Innocent and . . .'

'And cold! Look at them shivering.' But he was beginning to understand what she was worried about.

'We've talked about this before,' he said.

'I know, but it doesn't go away.'

'Martha, I've been thinking a lot about this. Our past doesn't go away. Like a scar, you know, but the hurt does. It's got to.'

She latched on to his last words. 'Scar, you said. That's just the problem.'

'What?'

'Stefan, I've got to tell you. I worry so much about it.' She took a breath and then she looked straight at him. 'I might be infertile. Why are you looking at me like that? Other women were. I heard them talking . . . I mean I didn't sleep around that much, thank goodness, and I hate the thought of those days, and you know God has been so good, giving me Helen and Michael and you, and your mother too, but I worry and worry about the consequences. It doesn't show, you know, but there are all sorts of problems.'

'Can't you see a doctor?'

'A doctor? You know how hard it is to find a good doctor in Koravia. Listen, it cost me everything to tell you all that and now you're talking to me just like – just like Thomas Niski!'

He tried again, 'Couldn't you talk to Helen about it?'

'I've thought about that. Perhaps I will if . . . well, she's got so many worries. I'll tell you something else. Perhaps you'll think I'm being stupid, but your mother's offered to give me her wedding dress. It's old-fashioned, but the dressmaker would re-make it, she said.'

'That's all right then.'

'No, it's not. Oh, Stefan, can't you understand anything? You know what colour a wedding dress is?'

'Of course I do, it's white.'

'That's exactly it. White like driven snow. Purity. Brides in white are meant to be virgins.'

'I'm sure most girls don't bother about that.'

'Well, I do.'

'White dresses are a waste of money.' Stefan tried to console her.

'Typical male commonsense!'

'What do you expect me to say?'

'Money's got nothing to do with it. Helen and I can alter the dress ourselves. Besides, brides are supposed to wear something borrowed, aren't they?'

'I didn't think you were so superstitious.'

'I'm not.'

'Yes, you are.' He broke off. 'Oh, Martha, don't let's quarrel.'

'We're not. I want our wedding to be so special – and you don't seem to understand.'

He gestured helplessly. 'Maybe I don't. I'm sorry.'

Why has it all gone wrong? he thought. Martha is always so sunny. She makes the best of everything. She doesn't usually let things get to her like this.

'Wait here,' he said, suddenly.

'Where are you going?'

He was running back towards the snowdrops, stooping down and pulling their stalks. She started to walk towards him. He straightened, holding the flowers.

'When we met in Tarnov Court at my trial, after not seeing each other for six months, you threw roses to me,' he said. *Roses*. In December. How can you say you have nothing to give? You mean everything to me, Martha. I know about your past, but that was then. You'd been pushed out of the children's home as soon as you were fourteen with nowhere to go except a grotty hostel. I got put into the hard men's section in the army. We were both forced into things. The difference is, I hurt other people. You just hurt yourself. When you said just now, why was I looking at you like that – I was thinking how wise you are. You're a year younger than me, yet you know so much more about things than I do.'

She was crying now.

'I'm sorry, Stefan. It's been so long, waiting for you, trying to keep cheerful.'

But Stefan hadn't finished with what he wanted to say. 'We know that what we did was wrong, but we know it's been forgiven,' he insisted. 'We've got to forgive ourselves. It's over now, for us. That's what I meant about not letting it hurt us any more.'

'I know,' she sniffed. 'It only makes it worse. I will talk to Helen,' she promised.

He nodded, 'I'm sure she'll help you.' He held out

the snowdrops. 'Will you marry me, Martha?'

She flung her arms round him. Fragile white flowers were bruised in their embrace. 'Wear your white dress, Martha,' Stefan said. 'You'll be the most beautiful bride in all Koravia.' He kissed her tears away and, arms about each other, they walked up the sunlit path. The birch woods about them were alive with birdsong and spring.

Martha gave her snowdrops to Adam Puls. 'I want him to share in the spring. Isn't he like Joanna?' she added, and aloud she said, 'Your daughter Joanna's very like you, Adam. Mind you, I think Sveta is too.'

'Sveta, aye, I haven't seen Sveta since she was a bairn. The wife doesn't want to bring her here,' the ploughman from Kostka said in his soft, slow voice. 'I've heard all about you, Miss Martha,' he went on in the old-fashioned country way. 'I appreciate everything you've done for my family. Our Joanna thinks the world of you.'

'I think a lot of you too,' Martha said, embarrassed. 'We all want you to come home.'

'Home, ah yes.'

But it sounded as if 'home' was a distant dream, and they sat in an uncomfortable silence, not knowing what more to say.

'I think we should go soon,' Martha ventured, finally.

Adam turned to them with those searching blue eyes that were so like his daughter's: eyes which had seen too much, thought Martha; eyes which knew how to look, guessed Stefan.

'Don't think because I don't talk much I'm not all here,' he said, and Martha blushed. 'I remember everything. I recognized you straight away, Stefan. You went through hard times because of me. I pray for you. I pray for Michael too. Now, there's a fine man!' His voice died away again and his blue eyes stared into some unknown distance.

'Come on, Stefan,' Martha whispered. 'We'll come and see you again, Adam,' she promised.

'Yes, come again,' he said and he held out his hands

almost as if he were blessing them. 'I had strong hands once,' he said. 'They've taken my strength away. They've taken everything away except the light.'

They stared at him. 'Come *on*,' Martha pulled at Stefan.

Stefan stooped towards the rickety hospital chair which seemed too flimsy for Adam's frame. He took Adam's wasted hand in his. 'Good-bye, Adam. We'll come again as soon as we can.'

Adam pulled Stefan to him and embraced him, kissing him three times in the Koravian way. 'God bless you both,' he said.

'He's not mad,' Martha decided once they were finally outside, 'but he's not quite sane either. They've destroyed something inside him. Do you think he'll ever be . . . well, you know, normal?'

'I don't know,' Stefan answered slowly. 'It's as if he sees things the rest of us don't.'

Martha shivered. 'His poor family!'

'I know.'

They walked along in silence.

'I keep thinking how Adam said everything has been taken away,' Stefan said. 'He isn't on the same plane as us any more. I can't put it into words, though.'

'He made me feel jittery,' Martha confessed. 'Let's hurry for the bus, Stefan. I don't feel like picking snowdrops now.'

On the way home Stefan said, 'I've decided on our wedding date.'

'When?'

'Pentecost.'

'Will it be in the barn in Kostka or a proper church building in Lipa?' asked Martha.

'That's not for me to say. Your choice, madame,' Stefan said grandly.

'Kostka, then,' Martha replied without hesitation, 'and Joanna will be my bridesmaid.'

'Shall I ask George to be best man?'

'George?'

'He is my only brother.'

'But he doesn't have anything to do with you.'

'I know. I'd like to ask him, though.'

'All right. I haven't anyone in the world, except Michael and Helen. Oh, Stefan, it would be a dream come true if Michael could be there!'

'There are plenty of other things to settle first,' Maria Cornelius said briskly, when they told her their plans at supper that evening. 'Things like a job and a room to live in.'

'I know,' Stefan agreed, 'but I've got a month before I start work. I'll go to Tarnov and stay with Thomas for a few days.'

'He seems to know everyone. He might help you find somewhere for us to stay. I'll have to get a job as well,' Martha said. 'Listen, what's that noise? People singing in the street.'

'Some drunks coming home from a party most likely,' Maria said.

'No, they're singing hymns.' Martha ran to the window and pulled aside the curtain. 'They've stopped right outside the house. Thomas Niski is with them.'

'Tell them to come in at once. Oh dear, if it's not one thing it's another. We don't want any trouble,' Maria sounded agitated.

Stefan and Martha hurried to open the door. 'Stefan, Stefan, welcome home!' voices called.

'But he is home!' Martha objected. 'You'd better all come in.'

'All of us?'

'Yes,' Maria appeared at the door. 'Better inside than out in the street. I'm sorry to sound so unwelcoming,' she apologised as a dozen or so young people crowded round the back door, 'but I don't want anyone to accuse us of holding a religious meeting.'

'No, of course, Mrs Cornelius. We can't stay long because of getting the train back to Tarnov, but we wanted to welcome Stefan home,' Thomas explained.

'This is Brother Leo,' he added, introducing a slightly built man of about thirty who shook hands warmly with Maria and Martha before he turned to Stefan with the traditional threefold kiss.

'Andrey and Thomas have both told me so much about you. We have prayed so much for you. It's good to meet you at last, Stefan.'

In the buzz of talk Thomas extricated Stefan and Leo.

'I'd like us to go next door for a few minutes so that Leo can meet Helen,' he explained, 'and, by the way, Stefan, I've brought you this.' Thomas pointed to a cardboard box.

'Did you carry that all the way from Tarnov?'

'We took it in turns,' Leo said.

'It looks like books.'

'Medical books. We thought they might be useful for you in your nursing,' Thomas told him.

'They certainly will! I want to go on studying, because I must do all I can to get back into nursing. Have you got any news about Michael?'

'Oh, Stefan, I wish we had!' Leo said. 'All I can do is offer Helen our appreciation and thanks.'

'She'll say the same about your sermons and prayers,' Stefan said.

'What a brilliant end to the day,' Martha declared as she and Stefan washed glasses and saucers after everyone had gone. 'Books for you, Stefan, and lots of hope for both of us. I liked Leo,' she added.

'He told Helen he attended Michael's trial,' Stefan said. 'Seeing Michael then, and reading Nik's letters changed his life. Andrey said the same sort of thing as well,' he started to tell Martha, but his mother interrupted as she ofen did when talk turned to topics she considered dangerous.

'It was very good of Brother Leo to come out to see you. I must say I was encouraged when I heard he might be able to get you a flat.'

'A room in someone's house, right in the centre of

Tarnov. It couldn't be better.'

'Now all we need is for me to find a job,' Martha said. 'I'd love to look after children, but there's probably not much chance of that.'

'I'm not given to optimism as you know,' Maria said, 'but these days so many surprising things are happening that you can never be sure. Perhaps something will turn up for you, Martha.'

'Perhaps,' Martha tipped washing up water away. 'I'd better go. I've got to start work again tomorrow. Still, Easter is only a week away. You know,' Martha added as Stefan saw her home, 'if only Michael were here with us we'd be the happiest people on earth.'

'It will be his third Easter in the coalmines – and who knows if he's even well enough to know it's Easter at all,' said Stefan. 'All we can do is pray.'

'It doesn't seem to make any difference,' sighed Martha.

'It makes all the difference in the world,' Stefan disagreed. 'You know that as well as I do.'

'I know I do really,' she admitted. 'Anyway we'll do our best to make Easter as nice as we can. Maria and you have to come round and eat in our house on Easter evening, remember. Easter evening,' she added, pausing on the doorstep. 'It has a magic sound all of its own.'

They were to remember those words when Easter evening came.

5

Dawn Flame for Koravia

Easter Day dawned cold. Martha and Stefan walked to church in a whirlwind of snowflakes. Their torches made pinpricks of wobbling light in the darkness, but in the east, over flat, frozen fields a glimmer of yellow light streaked the sky. It was five o'clock.

'Last year Helen and I went alone while your mother looked after Niki,' Martha recalled.

'And Andrey and I lit a stub of a candle. I tried to keep Easter for Michael. If only we could have some news!'

'I know; not knowing anything is grim. Look, Stefan, it's getting light. Do you see? In fact the sky over there is like a flame; and, listen, someone's ringing a bell. An Easter bell! In Kostka! It hasn't been rung for years. Hurry.' She broke into a run.

'We can't see where we're going.' Stefan's voice came in jolts as he jogged beside Martha.

'Follow the sound of the bell,' she panted. 'Oh, Stefan, I can't run any more. I've got a stitch.'

They slowed their pace.

'We're not the only ones following the bell,' Stefan commented.

In the dim light of early day it seemed as if the whole of Kostka village had turned out to celebrate the Easter feast.

People were muffled in winter coats. Everyone carried unlit candles, while the bell, silent for so long, clamoured from its tower.

'Wouldn't Adam be pleased?' said Martha. 'Perhaps

it's ringing for him,' she added. 'It must ring for Michael too . . .'

'It *is* ringing for them. It's ringing for us, and it's ringing for Koravia,' said Stefan as the sound of the bell swung through the waking day like an urgent flame.

Stefan and Martha squeezed into the crowded barn.

We rise at deep dawn to welcome our joy.

Their voices mingled with a swelling chorus.

All over Koravia churches would be as crowded as this barn. Maria and Helen would take Nikolai to the village church in Lipa. Historic stone churches in Tarnov would be so full that crowds would spill out on to the pavement. Teenagers would kneel in the streets. Carved country churches which Stefan had only glimpsed from prison vans or hard class railway coaches would be thronged; and, Stefan knew, far away on the building site, alone or with another like-minded prisoner, Andrey would be standing in drifts of snow, reading the Easter story in harsh light, while Adam would look out at bare trees and surely glimpse again the flame which had flickered through all the years of his long nightmare.

'There's Joanna,' Martha whispered, 'and Irene and the other kids.'

People were lighting candles now, one after another, bending forward to borrow light from their neighbour's flame. An orange glow spread through the barn.

Let the light be shining for Michael too, Stefan prayed. However dark it is for him, let there be light today.

'Alleluia!' Kostka's erratic choir broke into a wobbly crescendo. 'Christ has risen!'

'Christ has really risen!'

Their reply resounded through the rafters, while from the bell tower the flame of sound still jangled through the village.

'*Women sought you in vain with myrrh and with tears,*' sang the choir. '*But an angel shone like a flame before day.*'

Pressed close beside him Martha joined the singing,

but the hymn stirred memories for Stefan: memories of a punishment cell where he had been locked up with orders to 'rehabilitate' its inmate, a nameless prisoner who was serving a life sentence for anti-regime activity.

I roughed him up . . . he stood at the window singing Easter hymns. The other day I told Martha to forget about the past. She's right, we can't forget, and why should we? It was because of the past that we're here together now. I abused Michael, but he's never held that against me. He's only ever praised me, said things to me I've never deserved.

Candle wax dripped on to his hand. He shifted, but the barn was so crowded it was impossible to move. Amidst singing and prayers Stefan recalled Michael Laski's old-fashioned courtesy and gentle smile.

'You know all the worst about me,' Stefan had told him as they sat in the punishment cell together, the prisoner and the boy who had been put there to torture him. He could still hear Michael's reply, 'I see a brave young soldier who isn't ashamed to be kind.'

He sent me a note too, when we were both in prison before our last trial. He posted it between the grating which divided our cells.

'Once again you come into my darkness to be my encouragement . . .' The memory of those words had kept Stefan strong in his determination to support Michael through all the hunger strikes.

I wish I could still help him, Stefan thought. Kneeling in the barn where Michael and he had once milked cows, Stefan prayed desperately for his friend, while all about him candle flames guttered low and families and strangers sealed their Easter greeting with the three-fold Koravian kiss.

'You're very quiet,' Martha said on the way home.

'I was thinking about Michael.'

'Do you know, so was I. I wish he was home again.'

'Or at least that he was somewhere safe.'

'I'd rather have him home,' Martha said decisively. 'I've got you with me, and that's a dream come true, but we won't be complete until Michael's back. It's horrible that Niki's having to grow up without his father. We both know what that's like,' she added, 'but we mustn't say anything at home, though, about how much we're missing Michael,' she warned.

'Of course not,' Stefan agreed. After breakfast, while Martha and Helen got busy with preparations for the Easter meal they would eat that evening, Stefan took Michael Laski's son to the children's playground and shared his delight in an upturned stone, a stick to poke into the ground, the play of older children and the joy of being pushed through the air on a swing.

He took the little boy home high on his shoulders and read him stories until it was time for his afternoon sleep.

'Who's going to put you to bed?' Martha asked.

'Ne-fan,' declared Niki.

'Is he going to change your nappy too?' Martha teased.

'No, Martie do it,' Niki said.

'And that's the way it is,' Martha related when they were sitting round the table that evening. 'He likes Stefan for the fun things, don't you, Niki? Look at him now, sitting right beside you . . . but what's that noise?'

'Only a car stopping outside,' said Stefan. 'Sounds like quite a powerful engine,' he added.

'You're not expecting any visitors today, are you, Helen?' Maria asked.

'No, and I don't know anyone with a car in any case,' Helen said. 'Could it be George, do you think, Maria?'

'Not any more,' Maria said. 'George doesn't ride in big cars these days.'

'No, that's true,' Helen said. She gathered up dirty dishes. 'Now, who would like some Easter cake?'

'It took us ages to make,' Martha was quick to copy Helen's light voice.

How do they do it? Stefan thought. I know they're as jittery as me. We all know that only the police or the military have powerful cars like that.

His hands were shaking. He pushed them under the table.

'Is this the cheesecake you drain through a sieve?' he asked. 'It's definitely my favourite. I can't wait to have a piece.'

'Here you are then,' Helen began, but a loud knocking at the back door made her pause with the knife poised over the cake. Before anyone had time to move the kitchen door opened. Evening sun flooded through the opening and silhouetted the dark shapes of two uniformed men.

'Oh dear God, no!' Stefan overheard Martha's anguished whisper. His hands went out to her, but she snatched Niki into her arms and stood frozen to the spot as more shapes crowded round the opening.

Six, counted Stefan, silently, his arm around Martha.

Helen stood up. 'What is it?' she asked.

The men made no reply.

'In there!' a voice ordered. There was a scuffle. A man was pushed into the kitchen. He stumbled to his knees. The door slammed shut behind him. His hands went up to shield his face.

'Michael!'

Was it Helen's voice, or Martha's? He heard Martha's now, low and agitated, 'Niki's trembling all over . . . So am I. Oh God, oh God, I can't believe it.'

'Michael! It's all right, they've gone.'

'They've doped him. He doesn't know where he is. Michael, it's all right, there's no one here except us.'

Slowly Michael lowered his hands. Helen was beside him now, cradling his shaven head against her. Stefan ran forward and helped Helen lift Michael into a chair.

'Home? Have I come home?' he murmured, rubbing his face. 'But they said . . .'

'Yes, Michael, this is your home. Look, we're all here. It's Easter evening, and we're finishing our meal!'

'It can't be true. It's a trick. They said . . .' he began again, and a terrible, hunted look crossed his face. 'Where are they now?' he asked.

They looked at one another.

'We haven't heard the car go,' Martha whispered, still

holding Niki. 'Oh, Stefan, what have they done to him?'

'It's all too obvious,' Stefan said grimly.

Yes, some of it was obvious, he thought as he went through to the front room to look from behind the curtains out to the street. They've beaten him up, that's for sure, but what have they done to him mentally?

The police van was parked outside the house.

'They're still there,' he reported back, trying to keep his voice steady. 'They've switched the engine off and they're sitting inside, but the windows are dark. I couldn't make them out clearly.'

He squatted down beside Michael. 'You really are home, Michael.'

Slowly, Michael reached out an uncertain hand. 'Stefan?'

Are they going to take him away again? Is this all some terrible trick?

'Michael, it's all right. We'll look after you now,' was all Stefan could say, while his mother and Helen were already bustling around.

'A little of that broth, that's it, just a few spoonfuls. Here you, are, Michael dear,' Stefan's mother bent over her friend.

He tried to squeeze her hand.

'How kind of you! I know from of old how good your soup tastes.'

Stefan took the bowl and helped Michael eat. His face was bruised. His lips were dry and swollen. His teeth were very dirty and about him hung the prison smell Stefan knew so well: the smell of unwashed clothing, of an unfed, neglected body.

He's nothing but skin and bones, he thought, and was aware that Niki was standing watching wide-eyed as Stefan fed this stranger.

'That should be enough,' Helen monitored anxiously. 'Little and often just now, until he's stronger.' She bent down beside her husband and Stefan stood aside.

'Lena, my Lena,' Michael's cracked lips murmured.

'You're home, Michael,' Helen repeated, and it was

as though they couldn't stop saying it. 'Thank God you're safe.'

'What about the police car?' Martha whispered.

Stefan went back to check. 'It's still there,' he said. 'Perhaps they're only trying to frighten us and spoil Michael's homecoming.'

'That's just the sort of thing they would do,' Martha said, and Helen added, 'I'm going to forget about that car and enjoy the greatest possible gift we could be given: my husband is alive and has come home again.'

Michael clasped her hand. 'I too have received an Easter gift,' he said. 'In fact I told them that it would be so,' he added.

'What does he mean?' Martha whispered. 'Did he know he was coming home today?' And aloud she said, 'Tell us what you mean, Michael.'

They gathered about him, bending close to hear, all except Niki who played quietly by himself.

'It's best to let him take his own time to get to know his daddy,' Martha observed, but Michael was holding out his hand to her. 'Martha, now I hear your voice, I can begin to believe I'm really home. Are you well, my dear?' he added.

She nodded, unable to reply, and Helen spoke for her, 'Martha has been a wonderful support to me. I don't know what I would have done without her.'

'Niki too,' gulped Martha and, changing her mind about letting him take his own time, she scooped the little boy up in her arms. 'Niki, Niki, here is your daddy. Daddy has come home.'

As if in a dream Michael reached out to stroke his son's face, but he drew his hand back, 'I don't want to frighten him,' he said.

'He's got your curls, Michael,' Martha commented, and Michael smiled at that. 'If you say so, Martha.' But then his face sobered. 'May he never have them shorn like mine.'

'Like Stefan's too,' Martha said, trying to cheer him up. 'He's wearing the bristle brush style at the moment.'

'Ah yes, so I am in good company, and I must hear your story too, Stefan.'

'There's plenty of time,' Maria reassured him. 'You mustn't tire yourself, Michael.'

'No, but I want to tell you everything. What a wonderful Easter gift this is! You know, I told my guards that already twice during many Easters in captivity, I have experienced the touch of an angel. And now this is the third time.'

'When did you say that?' Martha asked.

He frowned, trying to remember. 'On Good Friday morning, when they took me away . . .'

'Took you away? Where?' Martha asked. 'Only tell us if you want to,' she added.

'Of course I want to, but there's something first. The soup, you know, no solid food.'

'He can't possibly walk to the toilet.' But with Helen and Stefan both well used to nursing that problem was soon solved, and Michael sat back in his chair and closed his eyes, gathering strength to tell his tale.

'Good Friday . . . and this is Easter Sunday . . .' he began and rubbed his hands over his face. 'Three days and two nights on the road, then . . .'

'You mean you've been travelling around in that car all weekend?'

'Yes, without stopping, except for necessary pauses at the side of the road, and then always in well chosen places, without landmarks in sight. The windows were dark. I had no idea where I was.'

'Did they give you any food?' Stefan's voice was hoarse.

Michael shook his head. 'Only water, twice I think. Could I drink now?' he asked.

'Here, Michael,' Maria immediately poured out warm water from the kettle and Stefan held the cup for Michael to drink.

'So they didn't tell you where they were taking you? Did they say what the purpose of the journey was?' Helen asked.

'Oh, yes. They were going to do away with me; they said so repeatedly.'

'They beat you, didn't they?' Stefan asked sadly. 'Did you try to escape?'

'I was in handcuffs the whole time. I think that sometimes, mercifully, I wasn't fully aware.'

'No wonder you looked so dazed when they pushed you in here!' Martha exclaimed.

'I'm sorry. I must have startled you.'

'*They* did, shoving in like that . . . but go on, Michael. You said you'd told them that you'd met an angel.'

'When they came into my cell on Friday morning . . .'

'Cell?'

'Punishment cell. They kept me in a freezing underground cell constantly in order to kill me slowly. By starvation, you know, and chronic sickness; but, as Stefan knows, the cold is always the worst thing to bear.'

'So it was true!' Helen exclaimed.

'You knew?' Stefan asked, and, looking at Helen, he understood why her hair had gone white.

'So what happened when they came into your cell two days ago?' Maria prompted gently.

'They put me into handcuffs. I said, "Why are you doing this to me?" They said, "Too many people know about you." Of course,' Michael interrupted himself to add, 'their words were insulting and abusive, but that is the gist of it.'

'Was that the first you knew about the way people were holding campaigns for you?' Martha asked. 'Stefan went on hunger strike three times for you, and they gave him three more months as a result.'

'But I came home in time for Easter,' Stefan said hastily. 'Yes, there's been all sorts of action for you, Michael.'

'I gathered that from their treatment of me. Indeed, they told me that I am their number one enemy and so they were going to take me away to a remote place where no malicious anti-Koravian agents would ever be able to find out what had happened to me.'

'Oh no! So they really were planning to kill you?' exclaimed Martha. 'How did you feel?'

'Very sad, but I remembered that this was the day of Christ's passion, so I said, "If I must carry my cross, so be it. I am in God's hands, not yours".'

Helen broke their silence, 'In spite of all their threats they have delivered you safely home.' Michael smiled at her and made as if to touch her hand, but dropped his back into his lap.

'It is the work of the Easter angel,' he said. 'I told them so, you know, as I have been trying to explain, only I am being too long winded.'

'No, you're not: it's just that we keep on interrupting. Tell us about the Easter angel.'

'The first angel, of course, was Stefan five years ago, who gave me bread instead of beating me. I shall never forget how wonderful that moment was, to be shown such compassion unexpectedly in that most friendless cell – and now I hear he has been going without food entirely for me,' Michael added, but Stefan only said, 'What about the other angel?'

'It happened last Easter,' Michael said. 'I was in the punishment cell then as well. There was a young guard on duty, a handsome boy, who was so cruel that everyone feared him. We used to say of him that he had the face of an angel but the soul of a devil. That day, though, when he came into my cell something made me give him the Easter greeting, Christ has risen.'

'What did he say?' asked Helen.

Michael smiled, 'Of course I expected a punishment, but instead he answered, "Alleluia, he has really risen" and the amazing thing is that for the next three days that young man tortured no one; and to me he showed great kindness!'

'That's incredible!' exclaimed Martha, 'But, do you know something: Stefan knew about it. Not in detail, of course. Don't you remember, Stefan? You were still in prison and you wrote to me that you thought Michael had been given an Easter blessing.'

'Is that so? I can well believe it. Stefan has brought me blessing more than once,' said Michael with a smile for Stefan.

'And just think what you've done for all of us!' Stefan returned. 'We prayed for you again this morning, Michael, but we never dared hope we would see you today.'

'Nor I, and of course when I told the guards about the Easter angel, they only jeered and mocked me,' Michael went on, 'but in the end, as Helen said, they were angels to me because they brought me home, even if it was with blows and blindfolds.'

'Blindfolds?' they repeated.

'So that you wouldn't recognize the house,' Martha guessed.

'So that I wouldn't see the firing squad, they said. They stopped the car and blindfolded me; then they led me outside, but at the last moment, right on the doorstep, as I now realise, they unlocked the handcuffs and removed the blindfolds.'

'They were trying to control you with fear, to make you their creature by means of deception of the most cruel kind,' Helen said. 'How thankful we must be that you are home. Do you know, Michael, dear, I think we should sing our Easter hymn and then these young ones should finish their meal. I don't think we should give you solid food yet, my dear, but would you manage a little more soup?'

'Just a spoonful,' Maria said. 'Don't try to stand up, Michael,' she added, but Michael insisted on standing to join with them in the Easter hymn which had echoed throughout Koravia that morning. Then Martha gave Niki cheesecake and bathed him in his own little tub. 'Say "night night" to Daddy,' she urged.

'How clean and fresh he is! Don't bring him too close, Martha,' Michael said. So they blew kisses. Then Martha and Maria stayed discreetly away while Helen and Stefan stripped off Michael's prison clothes and washed him. Helen brought neatly ironed pyjamas.

61

'I've even got toothpaste,' Stefan said. 'Wait and I'll get some.'

'Salt is fine,' Michael said, but Stefan hurried home and returned with vitamin pills as well as toothpaste. 'Presents from friends of Koravia far away in Ostrova. Do you want to go to bed now, Michael?'

'No, no, I shall wait and enjoy your company while you drink your tea and share your cake. Could I go and see Niki now that you have made me clean?' And as they helped him walk through the house, Michael's frail hands touched first Helen, then Stefan. 'Thank you both.'

The rest of the evening Michael heard their wedding plans and listened to their news. Later, they made up a bed in the kitchen for Michael so that Niki would be undisturbed and Stefan could keep watch beside his friend and ease his hours of fitful sleep. Daylight brought Martha into the kitchen, snatching breakfast on her way to work.

'That car stayed outside with its headlights full on all night,' she informed them, with her mouth full of bread.

'In that case I'll walk to the bus with you, Martha – if you don't mind me leaving you for a moment, Michael.'

'Of course not.'

As Martha and Stefan stepped outside the police car pulled away and another one drew up in its place.

'Do you think you should go back?' asked Martha.

'Let's just wait and see what happens. No, it's all right. They're not getting out. They're obviously keeping Michael under close supervision.'

The next few days would show how true those words were.

6

Light from a single flame

The police watched Michael day and night. Sometimes four, sometimes six, sometimes only two uniformed men were always on duty outside the wooden house where Michael was nursed by Helen and by Stefan, who was now at work in Tarnov, and came to Lipa on his days off with news of doings in the capital.

'Brother Leo is still preaching to packed churches. He had a letter from Andrey. It seems as if he might be released earlier than we thought.'

'I'm looking forward to meeting him,' Martha said. 'I'm sure he'll want to come here and meet Michael too.'

'How's your own work, Stefan?' Michael asked, from the armchair in the kitchen where he sat reading stories to Niki.

'Up to the elbows in puke. Do you know what they gave us to clean the toilets with? A toothbrush! I'm saying "us" because there's another guy in my wing, a friend of Leo's.'

'All the other orderlies are women, I suppose,' said Michael, looking up from the picture book.

'That's right. They tell me about their family problems, husbands who drink, kids who are in trouble. One woman's got a son who's on drugs. She said, "I wish he could meet you and Paul" – that's the other orderly. Paul says Leo has got some sort of centre going for kids like that. An old cellar. The police raid it, but no one seems to have stopped them from using it.'

'So good things are happening . . . that's the end of that story, Niki, see.'

'Again,' insisted Niki.

'No. Niki,' said Martha. 'It's nice and sunny. Let's go outside and play.'

'I'll come with you,' Stefan offered. 'I could see Michael was getting tired,' he said, once they were outside. 'It was a good idea of yours to take Niki out.'

'I didn't want to say anything in front of Michael, but with those guys watching all the time I'm frightened to let Niki out of my sight, in case they kidnap him or something. Do you know,' Martha went on as they found a patch of earth and sticks for Niki to dig, 'Michael made his first trip outside yesterday, just along the road with Helen, and they followed him the whole way, all six of them, quite openly. Everyone saw what was happening. They even stuck their heads in between Michael and Helen so that they could overhear everything they said. I don't like it, Stefan. I'm scared they're going to do something horrible.'

'I know, but Michael's so well known now that it would be hard for them to do much,' Stefan tried to comfort her.

The sun shone on Martha's dark curls. Stefan kissed the top of her head as she bent over the earth with Niki. 'Would you like to take Niki with us when we go to choose our wedding rings?'

She nodded. 'It would give Helen a break, and it would be so nice to have him too. We could all buy ice creams. I've just been paid so I'll treat us. Remember how you took me out for chocolate creams in that grand cafe in Tarnov? Some new shops have opened in Lipa now, the girls at work were telling me . . . Oh, yuk, Niki, a worm!'

Niki poked a fascinated finger into the ground and Martha's protests at his delight were ended by Stefan with a kiss which went on and on . . .

'For ever,' Martha said afterwards.

That afternoon they bought their wedding rings in a shop which belonged to an old friend of Stefan's family.

A small wooden cross decorated with budding willow hung on one wall. The elderly jeweller, who had supplied Helen and Michael with their wedding rings too, gave Niki a pile of coloured magazines to play with.

'It doesn't matter if he tears them up,' he said, taking out boxes of rings. 'A Pentecost wedding,' he went on as they bent over velvet trays and fitted one ring after another on the fourth finger of their right hands. 'Very suitable.'

'Because it's the start of summer, do you mean?' asked Martha.

'You could say so. It seems that light is returning to our country at last. Is that the ring of your choice, my dear? You've chosen well; it's old gold. The ring itself is not an antique but the gold is at least a hundred years old, bright as a buttercup,' he added, poetically.

'Then it's the best one for us,' Stefan said. 'My fiancée is fond of buttercups,' he explained, remembering something Martha had said once, and she looked up from the ring she had been examining to smile at him.

'Golden flowers, which brighten waste ground like you young Koravians,' the old man said. 'That's why I said a Pentecost wedding was suitable. Flames of fire, you know. You two simply don't realise the inspiration you are in Lipa. Your grandmother would be proud of you, Stefan,' he added. 'Now, allow an old family friend to present a small gift to the future Mrs Cornelius.'

He turned his stooped shoulders and disappeared into the back shop.

'What can he be doing?' Martha whispered.

'Something old, something new,' the jeweller's voice preceded him back into the shop. 'This is old, my dear, as old as the gold of the rings you've chosen, and I want you to have it with all my love. You've been a good friend to Helen and Maria and you've stood by young Stefan here through many harsh trials,' he went on in answer to Martha's protests. 'We'll let your bridegroom put it on for you,' he said, handing his gift to Stefan. 'There.'

'Oh,' breathed Martha. 'It's beautiful.'

An amber cross on a gold chain glowed on the palm of Stefan's hand.

'It's a little flame for our Pentecost bride,' the jeweller explained.

'I shall always wear it,' Martha promised. She gave the old man the traditional Koravian kiss. 'You must come to our wedding too,' she said, and he thanked her with an old-fashioned bow.

'So now you know how highly everyone thinks of you,' Stefan said as they left the shop and gave Niki swings along the rutted pavement.

'Of you,' Martha returned. 'What a nice old man! He reminded me of that old army officer who spoke up for Michael at the trial.'

'He was always on the right side, but quietly, you know. He was at Helen's wedding too, where you were the most beautiful bridesmaid ever,' Stefan told her. He swung Niki up on his shoulders. 'I had a letter from George; well, it was just a few sentences.'

'It's upset you, though, hasn't it?'

'I should be used to George by now,' Stefan said. 'And of course it was just what I expected. He doesn't want to be best man. He doesn't even want to come to the wedding.'

'I guess we both expected that,' Martha replied. 'I'm sorry though, for your mother's sake, as well as yours,' she added.

Dust blew around them, like dusty thoughts of dark haired George, the ex-army captain, who had served the regime from its earliest days.

'Perhaps we would never have been close,' Stefan said.

'He's certainly done you enough harm, writing lies in the paper about you and organising the whole arrest.'

'I know.'

George had had a hand in attacks on Helen in the early days, but Martha didn't know that. Better for her not to know, Stefan thought. She would find that very hard to forgive.

Had he forgiven his brother? He had thought so, during long months alone in prison, but Martha was right: George's rejection had hurt him, and, like a fool, rubbing his nose in this soiled relationship, Stefan had written back.

Dear George, I accept your decision not to be my best man, but I want to invite you to our wedding. Please accept this invitation for Mother's sake, even if you feel you don't want anything to do with me. I know I've caused you offence. I'm sorry. I chose my way, just as you chose yours. Perhaps it was chosen for us. I wish you well and hope that you will seriously re-consider your decision and that we will have the pleasure of seeing you at our wedding.

But George had not replied.

'Who's going to be our best man, then?' asked Martha. 'Thomas?'

'Do you mind? I know he's a bit stiff . . .'

'Pompous,' Martha supplied. 'No, sorry, Stefan, he's your friend, and he's been good to Helen and me too. Besides, I've got Joanna . . . and, best of all, we've got Michael back with us. Niki will be all dressed up too. Helen's made him a little embroidered shirt. So who's going to be all dressed up like his daddy?' she said, reaching up to Niki as he rode high on Stefan's shoulders. 'Oh, Stefan, do you know what I'm scared of? I'm frightened that they'll send Michael away for good; away from Koravia, I mean, and we'll never see him or Helen or Niki again.'

The black limousine parked outside the house seemed a sinister affirmation of Martha's fears, but inside the kitchen Michael greeted them warmly. Helen turned from the stove with her face glowing with good news.

'Adam Puls has come back home,' she said.

'I should dearly love to visit him,' Michael added, 'only I fear those shadows of mine may be too intimidating for him – but what is that beautiful cross you're wearing, Martha?'

So they told Helen and Michael all about their afternoon, and Niki added his information. 'Had ice-cream!'

he announced.

Hard on the heels of Adam's release, the authorities officially reopened Kostka village church for which the ploughman had endured drugs and imprisonment.

'In time for our wedding,' Martha told her friends at work. 'We're working day and night to get it cleaned up after so long.'

But still the police changed their regular shifts outside Michael's front door.

They even attended the wedding. As Martha walked on Michael's arm towards the newly opened church, two plainclothes policemen followed the bride.

Kostka church was crowded that day. The bell rang joyously from its tower and Adam, supported by some of the villagers, had a seat of honour, though he asked to leave the service soon after Martha joined her bridegroom at the front of the church.

Martha wore white as she and Stefan had agreed. Her dark hair was held back from her radiant face by a coronet of lily-of-the-valley picked that morning. Joanna held Niki's hand. He walked solemnly behind his father, obviously concentrating hard on his important page-boy role; and as soon as they stepped into church people started to clap. The applause continued as Martha and Michael walked up the aisle.

'It's for you, Michael,' whispered Martha, 'and you deserve it.'

'It's for you and Stefan too,' Michael assured her. 'I'm proud to be escorting you on your wedding day.'

'I'm proud too,' Martha replied. 'Nobody's wedding will ever be as special as mine!'

Now they were at the front, and Michael put Martha's hand in her bridegroom's. Rings were exchanged with promises and prayers. Thomas and a thin boy whose shorn head betrayed his recent whereabouts held crowns above the newly-married pair.

As they stood beneath their bridal crowns Michael stepped forward to speak to them. Everyone craned forward to hear what he had to say.

He was pale and gaunt, but his voice carried clearly through the crowded building.

'Today we witness the victory of faith,' he said. 'Our church is open. Prisoners are freed, all because, while things were dark in our homeland, faith still shone like a flame. The young couple whose wedding we celebrate are part of that light. As some of you know, some years ago Adam Puls saw light shine above this locked church. He reopened the tower and you know how he was punished. Stefan and Martha stood by him and his family, just as they stood by me. When I was starved and tortured in a punishment cell Stefan Cornelius disobeyed cruel orders in order to help me. He will never know how much light he brought into my life that day. Stefan has endured hunger and forced feeding for my sake, while Martha supported us all with unfailing cheerfulness.'

Michael held out his hand and Thomas Niski gave him two candles. 'Every young couple receives at their marriage a candle each to light from the flame which burns before the cross. Receive these candles, Stefan and Martha. Let them burn together from a single flame as a sign of your love for Jesus and for each other; for you are joined to Christ by faith and your marriage vows unite you to each other.'

They took the candles and Michael kissed them both. Someone started to sing quite spontaneously. All over the restored church voices took up the hymn. Stefan and Martha lit their candles to a surge of singing which continued as they walked down the aisle arm in arm and out into the village street where people jostled one another taking photographs of them, hugging, kissing and congratulating them.

'Martha, meet Andrey,' Stefan said, and the boy who had helped Thomas Niski hold the bridal crowns bowed. 'I'm pleased to meet you, Mrs Cornelius,' he said.

'So I am. I mean, I am Mrs Cornelius now, and I'm so pleased to meet you, Andrey,' Martha said. 'You've been such a good friend to Stefan. And have you met our bridesmaid, Joanna, and our page boy . . .'

'Michael's son,' Thomas explained as Andrey bent to exchange with Joanna the customary threefold kiss, treating her as an adult on this special day. He hugged Niki, and Stefan picked their little page boy up. Arm in arm, with Niki on Stefan's shoulders, the bridal party, followed by Maria, Michael and Helen and their guests walked towards the old barn where their reception would be held.

On the way Martha stopped outside Adam's cottage. Stefan opened the door, 'Adam, Adam, it's us,' he called. 'Thank you for our wedding. Thank you for sharing your vision of light. Martha's got something for you. She wants to give you her flowers.'

Adam shuffled to the door. Martha handed him her bouquet. 'Michael says it's all because of you,' she said. Adam shook his head. 'They've taken everything,' he said as he had done before. 'I doubt I'll work again. Perhaps my work is done.'

'Don't say that!' Martha exclaimed. 'Irene needs you and so do the children. Look, here's Joanna, and Michael wants to speak to you too.'

'And here is Michael,' a well known voice added, and Michael and Helen hugged Adam. The policemen watched, smoking, but did nothing.

'Are you coming to the wedding too?' Martha asked them, and there was laughter from people who overheard, because it was all too obvious that they would. 'Come at our invitation then,' she said firmly. 'This is our special day. You are fellow Koravians too. We invite you.'

They exchanged glances, stood up straight and bowed. 'Thank you, Mrs Cornelius. We accept,' they said, and so two plainclothes policemen joined in the dancing and stood with guests and villagers eating salads and sausage and soup.

'Everyone's happy, that's the main thing,' said Martha, as she waltzed round with the best man. 'I'm sorry George isn't here, for Stefan's sake,' she added, and it's a pity about Elizabeth too. We were hoping she would play a solo on her flute in church and maybe at the reception too.'

'Yes, she was sorry as well,' Thomas replied, escorting Martha back to her seat when the dance was over, 'But you know how things are. With this foreign tour which is coming up Elizabeth has too much to lose if she attends a wedding with high profile people like Michael and you.'

'Us?' laughed Martha, 'We're nobodies.'

'I wouldn't say that,' Thomas disagreed. 'Ah, here's Stefan.'

'We were talking about Elizabeth,' Martha said.

'Her foreign tour?' Stefan guessed. 'I always knew she had a great future with that flute of hers. She's going to Ostrova, isn't she?'

'I wonder if she'll meet that woman we know. What's her name again?' Martha asked.

'Dr Green,' Thomas supplied. 'Who knows? Official receptions will be arranged, but of course Elizabeth will have to be very careful who she talks to in a country like Ostrova which is outside our closed kind of political system – that is, if she ever hopes to be allowed to travel outside again, which, naturally, she does.'

'I'm glad I'm not Elizabeth,' Martha said as Stefan whirled her round in a traditional dance.

'I'm glad you're not, Mrs Cornelius,' he told her, 'but what I'm wondering is . . .'

'Yes?' she prompted him.

'When I'm going to have you on my own,' he told her. 'Let's go home, my own little wife and find out what marriage is really about.'

They left in a borrowed car which Thomas drove. Helen and Michael had already been chauffered home with a weary Niki. Maria left as well, for Stefan's mother was going to sleep at her neighbours' that night and leave her two-roomed house for the newly weds. No one was surprised that the two extra guests in well-tailored suits left the wedding when Michael did.

'Bye Joanna. Enjoy the rest of the wedding.' Martha hugged her bridesmaid. 'I can see how much you like Andrey,' she whispered, and Joanna blushed.

'He's nice,' she confided.

'He's too old for Joanna, of course,' Martha said to Stefan as they drove home. 'We're just like very important people,' she added, 'sitting in the back behind the driver.'

Thomas said goodbye to them at their front door. They stood on the doorstep waving. A car radio crackled and was silenced. '*They're* busy then,' Martha said. 'I wish I hadn't heard that radio. Look, your mother's opened the kitchen door. She's calling to us.'

'I'm sorry to trouble you, my dears, on your wedding night and at the end of a happy day, but you'll never forgive me if I don't tell you,' Maria said.

'What is it?' they asked.

Maria pulled the door shut behind her. 'We put Niki to bed and we were just having some tea and talking about the day,' she began, 'when Helen turned the radio on, for no reason at all. It was tuned in to World News from Ostrova and suddenly the announcer said, "News from Koravia. Michael Laski is to be deported with his family".'

'Deported? Are you sure? When?' Stefan asked. Martha said nothing, but he felt her tremble as he clasped his arm around her.

'Oh my dears, that's the dreadful thing, that's why I'm telling you now,' his mother said. 'Tomorrow morning first thing. They're packing a few things now.'

'It can't be true,' Martha whispered. 'Dear God, please don't let it be true.'

The gate clicked. They looked up.

'It's them!' Martha gasped. 'They're coming for them now.'

'Four,' counted Stefan – as if the number mattered.

Footsteps rang on the garden path.

'Go away!' Martha screamed. Her wedding dress

gleamed in the light of their torches. 'I won't let you come near them. Please, please, please,' she sobbed as the policemen strode past her, 'Please don't take Niki away. Oh, God, Stefan, it can't be true. They're the only family I have, apart from you. Oh, Stefan, Stefan, Stefan, say this isn't happening!'

Michael opened the kitchen door. 'Come in,' he said to the policemen, but he looked beyond them to his distraught friends. 'Martha, Stefan, come in.' His arms went round them and he drew them into the kitchen where Helen waited, white faced among the tea things.

'Michael Laski?' the policemen asked.

'Yes,' Michael replied.

'You are an enemy of our people. You talk about tortures and punishments. You incite young people to unrest and violence. You are a traitor to your homeland and no longer deserve to reside in Koravia.'

'No!' screamed Martha. 'It's not true.'

'Is there no possibility of appeal?' Helen asked.

They ignored her.

'A car will call for you tomorrow morning. You may take one small case and one item of hand luggage between you. Good night.'

Burly presences left the kitchen. The door shut behind them. Martha flung herself into Helen's arms and sobbed inconsolably.

7

'A brilliant send-off'

No one, apart from Niki, slept much that night. Stefan went racing back to Kostka.

'I'll let them know what's happened.'

'There's nothing anyone can do now,' his mother warned.

'I know, but we must tell them. They'll still be there, tidying up . . . Martha, love, don't cry,' he said, reaching out and touching her shoulder.

She shook him off. 'Leave me alone!'

He backed away, hurt.

'It's hard for us all,' Helen tried to comfort them. She wiped Martha's tears and pushed her damp hair back from her swollen face. Her wedding flowers clung limp and withered to her curls. 'Martha, listen, dear . . .'

'There's nothing to listen to,' Martha gulped. 'Nothing's going to make it easier. I can't bear it. I can't live without Niki.'

'I know, Martha, it's terrible,' Helen began.

'They're criminals,' Martha said. 'Koravia is governed by thugs with big black cars and radios.'

'They stop at nothing; we all know that. They would have killed Michael,' Helen reminded Martha. 'Go on to Kostka then, Stefan,' she added, 'but take care.'

'Go the back way,' his mother advised. She put her arms around her daughter-in-law. 'Do you think Michael and Helen could go on living the way they were, constantly followed and watched?'

Martha shook her head, 'But not to go abroad, not right away from Koravia.'

'He must. His life is in danger here,' Maria said.

Michael looked up from the stove he was trying to extinguish. 'We'll never be "right away" from Koravia, Martha. Our prayers will always unite us. Besides, it really seems as though night is ending. Dawn is on its way.'

'Then why are you being sent away?' Martha asked fiercely.

'Change is always slow,' Michael said. 'Some people say that there is no real change; that the beast of terror which has controlled Koravia hasn't been tamed; it has simply withdrawn its claws. . . . .'

'It's still got you in its grasp,' Martha interrupted.

Michael shovelled more ash into a bucket as he replied, 'No, dear, the truth is that we are in God's hands. He will look after us wherever we go.'

'I know,' sniffed Martha, 'but . . .'

'It isn't easy,' Helen said. 'It wasn't easy, either, when we came back to Koravia all those years ago and the police arrested Michael and Nikolai as soon as our train crossed the border; but you know how everything worked out in the end. I was thinking about that today when I saw you coming up the aisle on Michael's arm with Niki behind you.'

'Were you, Helen? Yes, I suppose you're right. I know Matusha . . .' Martha used the Koravian name for mother-in-law, 'is right too. You can't go on living like this, being followed . . . I want to go and see Niki,' Martha ended abruptly.

They let her go, and when Stefan returned from Kostka three hours later he found his wife in her wedding dress asleep on the floor beside Niki's bed.

'She cried herself to sleep, just like Niki does,' Helen said. 'I tried to comfort her. It's hard, though. But, Stefan, you're wet through.'

'It's raining in torrents outside,' Stefan explained.

It was raining next morning when a soft knock sounded at the door.

75

'It's them!' Martha said.

'It's not loud enough,' her mother-in-law pointed out.

'Would you like me to open the door?' Stefan asked.

'Yes, please,' said Michael. Their visitor was Thomas Niski, brushing wet knees.

'I climbed a few fences to get here,' he explained. 'I parked down the street and came round the back. We're going to give you a brilliant send-off, Michael,' Thomas enthused.

A brilliant send-off . . . How can he talk like that? Stefan thought; but at Thomas' suggestion he and Martha followed Thomas out across various back gardens into his car. They drove to the airport along deserted roads in pouring rain. Stefan sat in the back with Martha, holding her hand. She stared through wet windows, struggling with her tears.

'Here's the airport now,' Thomas broke their silence. He switched off the engine. The windscreen wipers fell back into position. Thomas got out into the rain to remove headlight bulbs and wiper blades. Leo and Andrey came to meet them. They were both carrying huge bunches of flowers and it was anyone's guess where they had got them from at that time of the morning.

Leo offered his bunch to Martha. 'Congratulations on your marriage,' he said. 'I'm sorry your wedding day had to end the way it did – but at least now we can stop being afraid for Michael's safety.'

'You mean . . .?' Martha began.

Leo shrugged. 'They have their methods.'

'I see,' she said slowly, and as they walked into the main hall, Martha said to Stefan, 'I'm beginning to see that it's the only way Michael will be safe. He needs medical treatment, and Leo's more than right about their methods. But, oh, Stefan, it's Niki, growing up so far away from me. He won't even remember who I am. Helen will show him photographs and she'll say, "That's Martha, a girl we knew when you were a baby. You were a page boy at her wedding".' Sobs choked Martha's voice.

76

Stefan put his arms round her. 'I know, Martha, I know,' was all he could say.

Thomas bustled across. 'There's a whole crowd from Holy Cross Church coming,' he began, but at that moment the police car pulled up outside.

Martha gave a shuddering breath. 'I can't bear this,' she whispered.

Stefan drew her close. 'Let's go and meet them,' he said.

A policemen blocked their path. 'Name?' he questioned.

'Cornelius,' Stefan began, but Martha stepped forward. 'Excuse me, please, we've come here to say good-bye to our friends. No one needs to give their name when they're seeing off friends at an airport.'

'Some friends,' he sneered. 'That man is a traitor, number one enemy of Koravia.'

'If you call Michael Laski an enemy I'd like to see who you think is a friend,' Martha retorted. 'You're doing a bad, wicked thing, sending away a family who can only bring good to Koravia.'

Stefan pulled Martha's arm, 'They're coming now. Mother's with them. They must have let her ride in the police car too.'

'That's something, I suppose . . . and, Stefan, look at all these people. Thomas was right as usual. Look, here's a good job for you,' Martha told the policeman. 'You'll be here all day collecting names.'

He turned round. Martha and Stefan pushed past him and ran towards their friends.

'Going on aerieplane,' Niki told them proudly.

Martha gave her flowers to Stefan to hold while she took Niki from Helen, 'Yes, won't it be lovely?' her voice quavered.

'Martie too?' he asked, and Stefan said hastily, 'Not this time, Niki.'

'Why Martie crying?'

'I'm not crying,' Martha said. 'Look at all those people. They've all come to see Niki go on the aeroplane.'

'Policemens here too,' said Niki.

'They sure are,' agreed Stefan grimly. 'They're trying to cordon off this whole section of the airport.'

'Let's ignore them for now,' Michael said. He put his arms round both their shoulders. 'That was a lovely wedding yesterday,' he told them. 'No wonder the sun shone so brightly for such a celebration! And now you're setting up house together, we want you to have our furniture.'

'Use everything, bed linen and crockery and so on,' Helen put in, 'Martha knows what's what, and, Stefan, my dear, we've left you our books.'

'Distribute them to whomever you think,' Michael added, 'and, it goes without saying, keep what you need for yourselves.'

'Flight number KA667 from Tarnov to Strandon, Ostrova.' A disembodied voice cut across their conversation. They strained to hear.

The police tried to regain control. 'This way,' an officer ordered, but Michael lifted a hand.

'One moment, please.'

'Whatever for?'

'We are leaving the homeland we love,' Michael began, and as they attempted to silence him, he challenged them directly, 'Is this showing a true spirit of open dealing and honest understanding, when you forbid us to take leave of our friends?'

'Oh, no, it's going to get rough,' Martha clutched Stefan's arm as two policemen lifted their batons, but just then foreign tour groups spilled over into the hall which the police had obviously been trying to keep sealed off. The police, all but two, melted away and the 'brilliant send-off' Thomas had described took place in an instant.

Koravian hymns resounded through the airport. Many people knelt to pray for the Laski family. Embarrassed guides tried to find acceptable explanations for curious foreign tourists as people pressed round Michael, kissing his hand and giving him and Helen and Niki the three-fold kiss.

Helen spotted Leo and introduced him to her husband. 'This is Brother Leo, Michael.'

Leo too kissed Michael's hand. 'Thank you, Michael, for your sufferings and faith.'

Michael drew Leo to him in a warm embrace. 'Thank you, Leo. I hear how crowds come to hear you preach, yet you are not afraid to align yourself publicly with me. I know I owe my release in part to you.'

'No, Michael, no. I want to tell you that the story of your return to Koravia over fourteen years ago with Helen and your friend Nikolai, his letters, your sufferings changed my life. I attended your trial,' he added in a rush. 'I knew I couldn't remain uninvolved. Pray for us, please,' he ended, and people round about begged, 'Don't forget us, Michael. Pray for us, Helen.' They pressed flowers on them, more flowers than they could possibly hold and a bag which bulged with presents.

'We are only allowed a case and a small bag,' Helen protested.

'Then we shall hand these presents to the tourists from Ostrova and ask them to give them to you when the plane leaves Koravian air space,' Leo said.

'Flight number KA667.'

And now the police intervened, trying to look unobvious and yet official. 'Michael and Helen Laski board now,' an officer said. 'Quickly, now.'

The crowd parted. Stefan pressed Andrey's ichthus fish into Michael's hand. 'A present from prison,' he said as Martha turned a face full of tears away from Niki.

'Martha, Martha, we are praying for our reunion,' Helen said. 'There are signs that the border may open,' she added, drawing Martha and Stefan to her. 'But however sealed the border nothing can ever shut out our love and our prayers for you both. God bless you both, dear ones. God bless you too, Maria.'

And now there was nothing more to say except a last, long embrace which no one could bring themselves to end. The police ushered Helen and Michael, two plastic bags, a small case, armfuls of flowers and a weeping Niki towards a sealed gate so that they would board the plane first and not have to mingle with groups of foreign visitors.

'Don't go,' Martha whispered, 'Helen, Michael, don't go.'

Stefan put his arm round her. Tears were streaming down her face. 'Niki!' she screamed as the gate swung shut behind them, but her voice was thick with weeping and the scream turned into a croak. She flung herself into Stefan's arms and wept against her husband's shoulder for a long, long time. Maria, Leo, Andrey and Thomas gathered around, organising lunch, a bed, transport, and Leo said something about working in a creche which neither Stefan nor Martha could take in. They never remembered leaving the airport, and only had the vaguest memories of being given tea, somewhere . . . Later, when they got to know Leo better, they realised it was in the parish house belonging to Holy Cross Church where Leo worked in Tarnov Old Town. Then there was a bed, crisply laundered sheets and sleep, clinging together, and waking hours later to turn to comfort one another with their lovemaking.

Ever afterwards they were to laugh together when they recalled that their marriage had been consummated, 'to use the correct term,' Martha always said, in a church house within sound of deep voiced bells which here, as in Kostka, had begun to ring again from gilded bell towers; a great tourist attraction, the authorities were beginning to realise.

They surfaced to normality and Martha's cheerful nature was the thing most of their friends perceived, but Stefan knew that the sorrow of that parting had left a deep scar in both their lives.

Michael had scars too, Stefan recalled, as he heaved furniture from the Laskis' house in Lipa up narrow stairs to the sunny room he and Martha rented right under the eaves of an Old Town house. They had to share a kitchen two floors down and a bathroom one flight of winding stairs below their room, but they had two windows looking over the steep gabled roofs and golden domes of the Old Town. Martha liked to face south towards Lipa. Stefan liked the west window which caught the evening sun.

Michael's scars. Years of prison, beatings, torture leave their marks, and Stefan had good cause to know how much Michael was marked.

'I thought nobody could be more beaten up,' Stefan said to Martha one July evening as the sun burnished domes as yellow as the corn fields which would be ripening in Lipa and Kostka; fields Adam Puls could no longer plant or plough.

'But when Helen and I undressed him last Easter . . .' he went on, 'Oh, Martha, he was almost a skeleton. I don't think there was any spare flesh on him, but there were scars, new scars and open sores that must have hurt him terribly, yet he never said a word.'

Martha nodded. She pulled a careful stitch in a shirt she hoped to post to Niki, but no letters had come from Michael and Helen, no address, not a word.

'I wish we could get some news. We can't send letters to them if we don't know their address,' she said, and Stefan knew without looking that Martha's gaze had gone to the photograph of Niki she kept on the old-fashioned small table at her side of the bed.

Two flights below a doorbell rang.

'Is that our bell?' Martha wondered. Those in the know would give three short rings, but Stefan was sure he had only counted two.

'I'll go and see anyway,' he said, opening the door.

Their landlady had got there first.

'Yes, upstairs,' they heard her say.

'It is for us, then,' Martha started to go downstairs. 'I'll go and put the kettle on, and I'll see . . .' her voice died away. 'It's the woman from Ostrova,' she whispered. 'What was her name again, Dr . . .'

'Dr Green!' Stefan exclaimed at the same time as their unexpected guest toiled up the last flight of stairs.

'It *is* you. I glad I at right address,' she gasped, trying to gather her breath and her Koravian together.

'We're glad too,' Martha said. 'It's nice to welcome you into our flat. You know Stefan, don't you?'

'Yes, we met once. He give me papers, I remember. How are you, Stefan? But first, dear friends, greetings from Michael and Helen.'

And Andrey, ringing the doorbell that moment on a chance visit to his friends, teased Martha afterwards at the beaming smile which split her face from ear to ear. 'All I saw was a huge smile with Martha running behind it,' Andrey said afterwards.

'Come in, Andrey!' Martha exclaimed. 'We're just going to hear news about Helen and Michael! You've come at the right time,' she added as she introduced Andrey to Dr Green.

'They well and happy. They send their love and wonder why you do not answer their letters.'

'Letters? What letters? We haven't heard a thing since they left,' Martha said, pouring tea, 'So it's doubly nice to see you.'

'Nice to see you too,' Dr Green replied. 'That beautiful cloth you sew me is always in my house. Helen noticed it.'

'Has Helen been to see you?'

'Oh yes, they live with me . . .'

'*Live with you?* You must write down your address.'

'Of course.' Once that was done Dr Green said. 'See, here are pictures.'

'Is that really all your house? It's as big as this one and four other families live here.'

'I know, I'm sorry.'

'Oh, there's Niki, playing in your garden. Please let me look at that one again.'

'Of course, you keep it.' And over tea and cake – 'made by Martha,' Stefan explained, they shared their news.

'Michael has been in hospital,' Dr Green said. 'He has now only one kidney. They diagnose diabetes as well, but the doctors are pleased with his progress. He and Helen will make a lecture tour later when he stronger.'

'With Niki too?'

'Of course. He has made you this.' She gave Martha an envelope with a scribbled drawing.

'From Niki? Oh, so he still remembers me! I'm sure he got more pen on his hands than went on the paper though.'

'They hear about your work with, how we say, boys and girls in trouble.'

'It's not so much us, it's brother Leo, but we're getting involved too,' Stefan said. 'But how did they know?'

'Network of friends,' Dr Green smiled. 'You are well known, both of you.'

'Of course they are,' Andrey put in. 'They just don't realise it. How long are you here for, Dr Green?'

'One week.'

'Would you like us to tell Leo that you're here?'

Dr Green smiled. 'Network of friends again. I see, no saw, Leo today. He is very fine.'

'Yes, he is,' Andrey agreed. 'Do you know how hard it is for him, Dr Green? He has been right through seminary. That's difficult enough, and he managed not only to survive without being corrupted, but to be given permission to work right in the middle of Tarnov. It's a miracle,' he added, but then he recollected himself. 'I'm sorry, Dr Green, only we know how much you do for us and we want you to understand everything about our life here in Koravia.

'Thank you,' said Dr Green. 'Please tell me.'

'Well, you see, our leaders talk about "democratiz-ation",' Andrey said. 'That's not the same as *democracy*, as Leo will tell you. There are problems when we do our club work. They make official pronouncements about trying to eradicate delinquency, drugs . . .'

'Drinking and divorce,' Martha put in. 'Not to mention AIDS.'

'I suppose every society has these problems.'

'Yes, and one positive sign of change here is that at last our government is beginning to admit that we have problems,' Andrey said. 'They're beginning to see that the church has something to offer too, though they still limit our activity. Preach nice sermons, yes, all right, but don't do anything positive, because that's stepping outside party control. I was followed home the other night,' he added.

'Followed home? That's bad. Was that from the club?' Stefan said, and Martha tried to explain it slowly to Dr Green.

'Do you think anyone noticed you coming here?' Andrey asked their visitor.

'I think not. I always look very carefully, besides we are now told that there may soon be a free exchange of visitors. Friends from Koravia may come, not just on official delegations but for holiday.'

'That's very new,' Stefan said.

'Yes, but the sort of friends they'll give visas to are people who toe the line,' Martha said, 'not anyone like us.'

'We shall see,' Dr Green replied. 'Look, now, I give you parcels. Only small things. I couldn't carry too big, and Helen and Michael not much money.'

'It's nice of them to think of us; and it's kind of you too.'

'No, nothing, my pleasure. But I surprise you don't get letters.'

'They're obviously still giving Michael "special treatment",' Stefan put in. 'It just shows what would have happened to him if they hadn't kicked him out.'

'I think so. Perhaps if you address your letters to me, not to them, they arrive safely. Now you must tell me your news too for them. You still work hospital orderly?'

'Yes, but I'm studying as much as I can, and Martha is working in a crèche. That's a nice piece of news.'

'I'm in the section for very small babies, tell Helen,' Martha smiled. 'I suppose they think it's all right to put someone like me to work with little ones because they won't understand if I try to teach them prayers. I don't mind. I say a little prayer every time I start work and when I put the babies down for their rest time I make a cross over each one and I ask our Lord Jesus to bless them,' she finished more slowly, making the appropriate gestures for Dr Green to understand.

'The crèche is in the Old Town,' added Stefan. 'A friend of Leo's fixed it up. Leo has friends everywhere,' he explained, but Andrey added, 'And enemies.'

'So tell Helen and Michael to keep on praying for him; and here's another piece of news for them,' Martha said. 'Our school year finished at the end of June, you understand?'

'I understand you very well, better than Stefan. I think you understand me better too. You know, women speak to small children. Talking to foreigners a little like that.'

'I always understood Niki perfectly,' Martha said, and a shadow crossed her face. 'I expect he's saying a whole lot more too.'

'Helen say, tell Martha Niki talks well. Better Koravian than me,' Dr Green smiled. 'Helen wanted write you letter, but we think better not. I carry letter, you understand, so she said tell everything. I wish I speak better for you.'

'You're doing very well,' Martha assured her. 'We always get on well, Dr Green. Remember the first time we met in the souvenir shop? You speak much better now, but we managed to understand each other then.'

'Good, so what's this other news?'

'It's Joanna. She's won a place in Tarnov Domestic Science School. She's very gifted.'

'Joanna lives too far away for her to be able to travel to Tarnov every day,' Stefan went on, 'and Adam still does very little, so Irene has a heavy time, but we all think, Irene too, that Joanna should take up her place, so after the summer she'll come and live with us.'

'Where she sleep?'

'Here. That armchair you're sitting on pulls out into

'a bed, just like the settee we use, see.'

'I see. Now, look, I go and you open parcels.'

'We must see you again, though, to give you things for Michael,' Martha said. 'You must tell us something about Ostrova too. You know that's our Koravian name for your country? It means 'island'. I've never seen the sea. What's it like to live on an island?'

'A lot of rain,' Dr Green smiled. 'Ostrova is quite a big island. If you live in the middle of it you can be quite far from the sea. Perhaps you will see for yourselves. Michael and Helen pray so.'

'We pray for them too,' Stefan said. 'And if we may, we should like to pray for you. We appreciate all you do.'

'I appreciate you,' Dr Green said. 'Our life is very different. You, how do you say, give heart to me. So, now, when shall we meet?'

They made their arrangements and when Dr Green had gone they opened their gifts from their friends and, to Martha's joy, found photographs as well.

8

Love transforms hardship to glory

They met Dr Green again and gave her presents for their friends: souvenirs of Koravia, a children's picture book. It didn't look much, but they both knew, and Helen and Michael would know too, that they had stood for many hours in queues for these things, although Dr Green herself could have walked into any one of the special foreign currency shops for tourists and bought such gifts at a fraction of the price.

Perhaps Helen and Michael would guess, though they hoped not, that they had spent most of their month's money as well.

'But it's worth it,' Martha agreed afterwards.

'Uh,' Stefan assented from inside a thick medical book.

Martha sighed and went across to the window. The late afternoon sun had worked its way round to the towers of Holy Cross Church. In Lipa it would be shining into an empty house where a little boy had played . . .

'I wish we were back there,' Martha said.

'Where?'

'Home. Oh, Stefan, I'm sorry, I shouldn't talk while you're studying. I know how important it is for you to pass that exam, but I miss them so much.'

'I know.'

A bell rang from the tower.

'I might as well go to the Transfiguration Day service,' Martha said. 'I've cleaned our room and I made jam from those berries Matusha gave us. Perhaps when

Joanna comes I'll have some company,' she added as she tied her scarf round her hair, but Stefan didn't answer. Martha sighed again as she went outside.

High buildings hid the sun. People pushed by, hurrying to get late shopping done on their way home from work. Trams and buses were already crowded. So was the church. Martha queued to buy a candle and added another flame to the ones which burnt in a circular stand.

Receive these candles . . . light them together from a single flame . . .

It's a single flame all right, Martha thought. Stefan is always too busy. His working week is so long, fifty, even sixty hours sometimes, and then he goes to the club with Andrey. Or if he's at home he's busy studying. Marriage isn't a whole lot of fun.

She tried to push those thoughts away as singing soared through the building.

Would Michael and Helen take Niki to church today? But perhaps it wasn't a holiday in Ostrova. Dr Green had explained once that churches there were different, and even if it were a special day, the service wouldn't be in Koravian.

Prayer opens closed boundaries . . . Michael and Helen both believed so. Martha made the sign of the cross. 'Please be with them, Lord,' she prayed. And with Niki, her thoughts went on. His little baby curls will soon be needing a proper cut. I was going to do it for him . . .

'Give us faith to glimpse the glory of the Lord in harsh times and lonely places.'

Martha looked up. The speaker was Leo. Around her people shifted, coughed and grew still.

'Love turns hardship to glory,' Leo said.

I believed so once, Martha thought. But it's hard when Stefan's always so busy, and I haven't anyone to turn to.

Leo was still speaking: 'Look about you at the candles you have lit. Those candles express your faith in the kingdom of heaven and your love for our Lord Jesus.

People talk about the changes which we see around us in our society and then they grumble because life is as hard as ever. We forget that we are given the glimpse of Christ's glory at his transfiguration so that our suffering may shine.'

Martha's head was beginning to spin.

Suffering . . . that was there, in prison, and afterwards, when Stefan was locked away, when we worried about Michael. But that's all over now . . .

More and more people were crowding into church. Leo was blessing them. Martha could just catch sight of his raised hands. Clouds of incense drifted through the packed building.

'May the light of Christ transform our lives into his glory.'

The choir turned the words into melody. The service would continue for a long time yet. A hand touched Martha's arm. She turned her head.

'Stefan! Stefan, I'm so glad you've come!'

'I should never have let you go out like that alone. I didn't even say goodbye.'

'You've got to study,' Martha whispered back. 'I don't know what's wrong with me. My head's spinning round. I feel horrible.'

'Do you want to go outside?'

'Mm. Do you mind?'

It was easier said than done. Martha clung on to Stefan as he shouldered his way to the door.

'Are you all right?'

'I'm okay, especially now you're here.'

'I leave you alone too much, don't I?'

'You can't help it, but I feel a bit trapped sometimes. Rooftops and pavements and traffic everywhere. I miss our village. I used to come home from work and Helen was always there to ask me how I'd got on. And of course there was Niki. I would pick him up and cuddle him. He loves cuddles, Stefan. He'd put his chubby little arms round me and hold on so tight . . .' Martha struggled with her feelings. 'It's kind of Dr Green to have them living with her.'

'Mm. You look a bit better now.'

'Yes, perhaps it was just the crowds.'

'And the heat. You'd been standing for a long time too.'

But a week later, Martha realised why she had felt so unwell.

She told her mother-in-law about it, back in Lipa on her next day off.

'It's early days. I mean, I've only missed once . . .'

'Oh, Martha, you're not pregnant, are you?'

She nodded. 'We're so pleased. Aren't you glad too, Matusha?'

'Of course I'm glad, Martha. I'm sorry if you thought I wasn't. It's just, well, you don't have much room and what about Joanna, now?'

'She'll be good company for me. Stefan works so hard. He sat his nursing exam yesterday. He wants to get back on the course, and then there's the club too. It's tough there. It brings back too many memories, I guess. There is one girl, though, her name's Hannah. She said she'd come up and see me sometimes.'

'You've got more than enough to think about. Have you been to a doctor?'

'Not yet. You know what it's like – bribes and everything.'

'Stefan should have been more careful, but you're at the best age for having babies so I'm sure you'll be all right, and I'll do everything I can to help you . . . like some vitamins. These plums come from Helen's trees. Wouldn't she be pleased at your happy news! Here, dip them into sugar first in case they're a bit sour.'

Maria gave Martha more plums to take back home. 'And news for Stefan from George. Bad news, I'm afraid. I phoned his old flat. He isn't there any more. He's in a rented room. Wait a minute, I'll get the address. Yes, here we are, Victory Square. I wrote to him. He sent a note back. It came this morning. He's not in the army any more. I don't know what's gone wrong. All sorts of reasons, I expect.'

Martha nodded. 'Poor Matusha. You must miss Helen too.'

'Oh, I do. She's my oldest friend. She spoke up for Stefan, you know, and got into trouble for it. You're still wearing your amber cross, I see – and that reminds me, that old jeweller has some relative who's a doctor in Tarnov. I'll find out more about that for you.'

'So Mother was all right?'

'She's fine. We talked about the baby, of course. She thinks you should have been more careful. It's not so easy, though, is it, Stefan? I mean the only way people here can limit their families is having abortions. One woman at work had her sixth last month. I told your mother about your exam, as well, and I said things were tough at the club.'

'You didn't say about the way Andrey and I have been followed, though?'

'No, of course not. I didn't want to worry her. She's got enough troubles. She misses Helen. It's horrible, that empty house next door. She's worried about George as well.'

'Perhaps I should go to see him.'

'Would you even know what he looks like?'

'I might not have done if it hadn't been for the fact that he arrested me. I don't think I'll ever forget the way he looked then. You can't understand that, can you?'

'No, but then I haven't got any brothers – none that I know about anyway. Are you going back to the club tonight?'

'Would you like to come too?'

'I'm not sure. I said to your mother there are too many bad memories. I mean, I meet kids who are, well, you know, on the streets and everything, like I was. I suppose that should make me feel lots of pity, and it did at first, but now I feel I want to forget about the past. We've got our own little baby to think about.'

'Of course we have. So, what would you like to do?'

'Are you offering me a whole free evening?'

'All two hours that are left. It's nine o'clock.'

'There's still some sunshine left. Let's find a park and look at green things.'

They went outside together, arms round each other in the August sun.

'The whole point is,' Thomas Niski argued one wet Saturday afternoon at the beginning of October, 'until they change the laws on religion in our country nothing is going to improve. It's all just cosmetic.'

'You mean, they've got to stop treating us like criminals?' Martha said.

'Criminals – and at best second class citizens. They open a few churches. They ease up some of their pressure, but what real difference does it make when people who admit to religious beliefs are discriminated against? Look at the trouble you were in last week, Joanna.'

'She can't hear you with those things round her head.' Martha reached over and raised one of Joanna's earphones from a personal stereo Thomas had wangled from a friend of a friend. 'Thomas was talking about the trouble you were in at Domestic Science School.'

'You don't have to shout,' Joanna protested. 'I can hear you. Trouble . . . well, it's not the first time.' She returned to her music.

'It certainly isn't,' Stefan said, 'but what's the point in discussing it even? Nothing is going to change. However well Joanna does in her course they won't let her go on to college because she's not in the Young Progress Corps.'

'It still shouldn't mean that her teacher threatens to throw her out for not joining,' Thomas argued.

'Of course it doesn't but "shouldn't" and reality are two different things,' Martha said. 'We have to live with the reality. For instance, even though Stefan's passed his exams, they may not let him back into nursing. There's the doorbell . . .' she interrupted herself, and while Stefan went downstairs to open the door, Martha added, 'I guess it's just what Leo said – we have to keep on believing, even when things are tough for us.'

'People abroad think our regime suppresses the church because our government believes in atheism, but the fact is the church is suppressed because it represents an alternative voice in a totalitarian regime,' Thomas was arguing as Stefan came back with Andrey.

'Come in, Andrey. Thomas was just getting all political,' Martha said. 'What's the matter? You look grim.'

'It's Leo. He's had both legs broken in a car crash,' Andrey said.

'When?' asked Martha, and, 'Was it an accident?' Thomas asked.

'It happened yesterday afternoon – of course it wasn't an accident.'

' "They have their methods",' Martha quoted Leo's own words. 'Oh, but is it never going to end? First of all Adam, broken completely with drugs . . . Then they try to murder Michael. Now this . . . I don't think I can take any more.'

'I'm going to phone Dr Green,' Thomas said.

'Your call will be monitored.'

'I'll do it, then,' Andrey said. 'They haven't anything on you, Thomas. It's better if you keep in the clear.'

'Where's Leo now? Can we go and see him?'

'Yes, if you want your names taken down. He's in the parish house . . . There are two police cars parked across the road.'

'Let's all go,' suggested Joanna, who had switched off her stereo. 'If there's a whole crowd they may not take names.'

Stefan and Martha exchanged glances. 'Joanna's right,' Martha said. 'We've got to try. Perhaps we won't be the only ones. Leo's well known throughout Koravia now. Listen, what's that?'

'Sounds like a choir singing. Is there something on in Holy Cross Church?' Thomas asked as they gathered up their coats.

'Not that I know of. Anyhow, you wouldn't be able

to hear it from here. Come on then.'

They went outside. Joanna and Martha walked arm in arm under an umbrella. Autumn leaves floated in puddles and drains. The noise of singing grew louder.

'Hymns. Something must be happening. It must be for Leo.'

They turned a corner towards the white walled parish house which held such memories for Stefan and Martha.

'Look at this!'

A huge crowd pressed outside the door of the house. Banners with texts from the Bible wavered in the rain. Many people were kneeling, regardless of the wet. Unaccompanied voices sang Koravian hymns.

'It's like when we said goodbye to Michael,' Martha whispered.

'There's Leo, look, on the first floor, where the window's open, and there are the police cars. Six now. Windows shut . . .'

'Who cares about the police?' Thomas exulted, shouldering his way through the crowd, pushing them closer to the parish house where Leo supported himself on two crutches. 'They're powerless against this.'

'Light candles for Koravia,' people were singing. 'Light candles of freedom,' their hymn went on. 'Freedom, freedom,' chanted the crowd. 'Perfect love drives fear away,' proclaimed their banners. 'Prayer and love will set our homeland free,' the people of Koravia sang.

Stefan glanced round him. The men were all bareheaded. Rain streamed down their faces but no one showed signs of wanting to move. 'Stay under your umbrella,' he said anxiously to Martha, and she nodded, but she was singing too, and so was Joanna, and there was no need now to make phone calls to Ostrova to Dr Green, because on the edge of the crowd, pressing closer, reaching the parish house, clinging to window sills for a better view were foreign reporters.

'A mass demonstration on behalf of the popular parish worker known as Brother Leo,' reporters noted in a dozen different languages.

'Not Koravian, though,' Martha commented afterwards. 'That's not the sort of thing our papers report.'

Martha was right, but Koravia couldn't silence the world's press. Television programmes suddenly featured little-known, closed Koravia. 'The eyes of the world are on Koravia,' commentators noted. 'Can the regime answer this amazing demonstration? Where will all this end?'

For the crowd outside Holy Cross parish house the demonstration ended as sirens wailed. Screams tore the air. Banners were discarded. Tear-gas ripped the crowd apart.

'To church!' people shouted. 'Leo! We are waiting for you in church.'

Stefan clutched Martha's hand. 'All right?'

She was clinging on to Joanna. 'Yes, come on, let's go too.'

Running, ducking, dodging, pushed and shoved, somehow avoiding the terrible explosions of gas, they crowded into the church, pressed too tightly together to breathe, wet bodies starting to steam.

'Prayer and love will save our homeland,' the singing continued, until cheering broke out as the slim figure of Brother Leo swung between two crutches. Unable to kneel, he prostrated himself. People pushed forward on to their knees. 'Let us pray for our homeland,' he said.

'And that's how it began,' Thomas and Stefan told a visitor from Ostrova, a friend of a friend of Dr Green, two months later. 'Now there's a special litany for the homeland on the last Saturday of every month. Actors and musicians join in, and Leo preaches. People start arriving at least an hour beforehand and there's never enough room for everyone who wants to fit in.'

'It all came out of their attempts on Leo's life,' Stefan added. 'If you can get news to Michael and Helen Laski, please tell them that especially. They will say it has to do with the victory of the weak, which is the only victory they believe in.'

'The victory of the weak,' their friend repeated in his

foreign sounding Koravian. 'People in my country are too often concerned with power. I think that is one reason why the prison letters of Nikolai impressed us so much. Like Michael Laski, he too faced failure, and yet his faith could look beyond his hopeless plight. It seems this litany you talk about is the same kind of thing.'

'We never thought anything good could ever come out of the bad times which Nik, Michael and, really, all Koravia went through,' Stefan told Martha later. 'But it seems, after all, it has.'

'I guess so. I tell you one thing. Leo has a really good thing going with all those musicians and actors taking part in his litany on Saturdays, but we never see Thomas's sister Elizabeth there, even though she used to play her flute in church,' Martha said.

'No, that's true, we don't,' Stefan nodded. 'Well, I said I'd go along to the club tonight. You don't mind, Martha, do you?'

'Not nearly as much as I used to, when you were studying as well. I've got Joanna to keep me company – when she isn't wearing her deaf aids,' she added, nodding at Joanna who was knitting and listening to earphones. 'She's doing what I should be doing – making Christmas presents. This time last year, we were making things for you. Now we're making baby things – and all you've done is make the baby!'

'You had your share in it too,' Stefan pointed out.

'Joint production. Do you think we fulfil the norms?'

'You more than fulfil my norms, anyway,' said Stefan, and out of sight of Joanna, they shared a goodbye kiss.

'I love you, Martha. You're the best possible person for me.'

'Funny – I could say the same about you. Go on then. I'll see you later.'

'I'll have to go now,' Stefan told some of the boys later above the blare of an antiquated juke box in the cellars where the club still met.

'Where are you hurrying to, Stef? Pubs don't shut for hours yet.'

'He has a lady – a real nice one too.'

'How do you manage it, Stevie?'

'There's no accounting for tastes,' Stefan told them, 'On her part, I mean,' he added, pulling on his coat. He hurried off into the December night.

Mist swirled around the old buildings. A few drunks staggered by. An old woman came out from a front door of some official building and started to sweep the steps with a birch twig broom. 'Disgraceful, that's what it is, disgraceful,' she complained, directing her broom and her disapproval towards a huddled shape on the pavement. Stefan muttered something in reply and was about to hurry on, but the shape looked familiar.

'George! Are you all right? George!'

Last time it was me on the ground, not him. 'George, it's me, Stefan.'

'Leave me alone,' his brother grunted, and slumped back down on to the frosty pavement.

9

Out of the Shadows

'Try to stand up, George. You'll freeze here.'

'Beat it.'

Stefan stood out in the roadway: 'Taxi!'

The driver of the taxi he hailed showed no interest and drove past. Besides, he had no money. He gave up and went back to his brother.

Two police swung by.

'Having trouble, comrade? We'll put him in the lock up, if you like.'

Their threats penetrated George's befuddled brain. 'Lock up . . . hero of Koravia . . .'

'He'll be all right,' Stefan said hastily. 'I'm taking him home.'

'All right then,' the more senior man said. They marched on while George spewed half a week's pay and a night's alcohol on to the icy pavement.

'Who's supposed to clean that up now? You should have stood him against that bin,' the old woman complained.

'I'm sorry,' Stefan apologised. 'Have you got anyting to clean it up with?'

'Course I have. That's my job. A cleaner. And my man drinks all the money I bring home. Drink and fighting at home, drunks in the street. "Clean it up", says the young master.'

'I'll do it, not you.'

She stared at him.

'You're not one of those young hooligans who go to that Holy Cross club then? They give the place a bad name. No wonder the police chase them.'

'I was there tonight,' Stefan said, kneeling down and starting to scrub.

'Never seen a man do that before. You're not drunk, are you?'

He shook his head, glad of the frosty air and the smell of carbolic.

George groaned and clutched his head with a muttered curse.

'A holy young man like you doesn't keep very good company,' Stefan's elderly mentor observed.

He wrung out his cloth. 'Who says I'm holy? Anyway, here you are, mistress. I hope that's clean enough for you.'

'Oh yes, that should do. Are you a believer then?' she persisted as Stefan emptied dirty water into the gutter and returned the bucket.

'Yes.'

'That's what I thought. No one else would bother. Wait till I tell my old man. We never go to church ourselves, like. No time. At least that's what he tells me, but I don't know. I think it would do us both good.'

Stefan nodded. 'Thank you for the hot water and soap, mistress.'

'That's all right.' She waddled away, and Stefan turned back towards his brother.

'Come on now, George. I'm taking you home.'

They slithered over icy pavements to Victory Square. Martha will be wondering what's keeping me so late.

'Do you have a key, George?'

'What for?'

'Your flat.'

'You always were an idiot. Course I've got a key. What do you think? Or are you spying on your own family now? You must have had inside information to know my address.'

'Mother gave us your address,' Stefan began. 'We're sorry you didn't come to our wedding.'

'Your wedding? I know what kind of wedding that

was. Some of the biggest criminals in Koravia were at that wedding, I heard.'

That's a matter of opinion, Stefan thought.

Ill-lit archways opened off the hallway of what had previously been a beautiful mansion house. The smell made it all too obvious what those once grand pillars were used for now.

'Listen, little brother, you can stop doing your love your neighbour act and get lost.'

'Can I come and see you again?'

'Typical. Can't see where he's not wanted.'

'I can see that only too well, George. Let me make you some tea or something.'

'Or something. Stronger stuff for me. Maybe that's what you're after too. I'm at the bottom now, kid brother, right in the pits, exactly where you've been for years. The difference is that you put yourself there and I've been pushed out by a load of lies. Betrayed, that's what happened. The Judas kiss. Someone I helped up the ladder pushed me off. Now you know.'

'I guessed, from things Mother said.'

'So that's the way of it. "Poor George", eh? I know what you all say. "He had such a bright future and now he's thrown it all away. What a failure!" And he *is* a failure, little brother, but don't let's admit it. Let's keep the stiff upper lip, the army officer on parade.'

'George, you know that sort of talk doesn't mean anything to me.'

His brother stared at him. In the dim light their eyes met for the first time.

He's heard me at last, thought Stefan. He's seeing me too, really looking, like he did that last time. He knocked me to the ground. He used his whip on me and we looked at each other . . . like brothers.

'How you must hate me,' said George.

'I don't hate you, George. I want you to come home with me and meet my wife. Did you know we're going to have a baby? A grandchild for Mother, and a niece or nephew for you. You can't cut us out of your life completely.'

'So that's it. "Let's keep in with Uncle George".'

Stefan's next move surprised them both. He put his hand over his brother's mouth. 'You know that's not true. We're happy, Martha and I,' he said, dropping his hand again. 'We want you to be happy too.'

'Don't be so pathetic. 'Happy? In Koravia?'

'Yes,' said Stefan firmly. 'Happy in Koravia. And now you're going to open your door and let me in.'

'So that you can gloat over the hole I live in? I had it good once, little brother, big cars, women, access to the best shops.'

'I know all about that,' said Stefan. 'And I know how it stinks, George, because in our country you acquire a cushy life by riding on someone else's back. Judas kiss, you said. Thirty pieces of silver. A prisoner gave me an orange once. That meant more than if it had been real gold. But I turned my back on it. I played it hard as well, didn't you know? I'm sure you were told about my progress through the ranks.'

'Yes, I was told, and I heard when you threw it all away.'

'They didn't tell you why, though, George, did they? Still, never mind about that now. It's late. I must go home and you need to get to bed too. Will you come and have a meal with us?'

'You really mean that, don't you?'

'I really mean it, George.'

'We'll see, little brother, we'll see. It's not as easy as you think. When you're drowning in a foul muddy pool it's hard to climb out on dry land. Perhaps there isn't any dry land, either.'

'Perhaps not – but there are bridges.'

'Quite a philosopher. Well, I'll not make any promises. Go home to your wife, little brother. Good night.'

But, as Stefan walked away, he heard his brother's voice. 'Wait a minute.' Stefan turned round. George was standing a few steps higher up, already trying to put his key into its lock. 'Do you really not hate me?' The hoarse words floated towards Stefan.

'No, George, I don't hate you.'

His brother nodded. 'That's all right then.' His hand gestured towards Stefan. An elder brother's blessing? Reconciliation? Or just a drunken wave? Stefan couldn't be sure, but as he pushed open heavy double doors and breathed in fresh air after the unsavoury hallway, a shadow fell across his path.

'Going home now, are you, comrade?'

What does he want? Is this just a provocation? Was the whole thing with George some kind of trap? No, the vomitting was genuine. Don't be afraid. Don't show any kind of fear. He pushed his hands into his pockets. It isn't always so easy to stop them shaking, but at least let them not be seen. He swallowed. His throat felt dry. Being followed was so often just the first step; and I don't want to walk that way again, not with Martha pregnant, not with a baby on the way.

He tried to speak calmly, 'Yes, I'm going home. Why?'

'No reason, comrade, nothing.'

'That's all right then.' He started to walk on at a brisk pace, but he knew without looking that the shadow was still on his heels.

Should he tell Martha? No, not this time. Perhaps it's a one-off thing. There's only one of them. Usually they follow in twos – or more. Perhaps with all this new openness they're short of a job. What was it he had written to George? *I chose my way, just as you chose yours. Perhaps it was chosen for us.* Perhaps it was . . . perhaps it was.

'He followed me the whole way,' Stefan told Andrey later. 'Don't say anything to Martha, will you?'

Yet was it right in a marriage to keep things from your wife? He told her everything about George at any rate.

'I don't know, Stefan. I mean, it would be nice to think that he's seen through the system. All that about can you be happy in Koravia – but he may still try to make trouble for us, even if it's only to win his way back to favour. But I'm sorry, I shouldn't say bad things about your brother. Listen . . . Feel.' She put his hand against her swelling middle.

'What?'

'The baby. It's kicking. Can't you feel it move?'

'No, but I can see in your face something special is happening.'

'Oh it is, it's the most beautiful thing. It was just a faint fluttering at first, but it's quite strong now. There, it's moved again. Joanna can feel it, can't you?'

Joanna looked up from her studying. 'I think so. Have you thought of any names for it?'

'Not really . . .'

'Oh, Stefan, how can you say that? You know we decided that if it's a boy we're going to call him Michael.'

'What about if it's a girl?' asked Joanna.

'I'm not sure. We still haven't quite decided,' said Martha.

Yes, in a few months time the little life which wriggled inside Martha would be a fully formed baby, no longer an 'it' but a 'he' or a 'she' who would cry and laugh, need space to sleep and play.

'Perhaps we should put our names down for a bigger flat,' Stefan said.

'And be stuck in an apartment block surrounded by concrete and probably put beside difficult neighbours. It's so nice and central here,' Martha argued. 'It's just a nuisance we have to carry our meals up two flights of stairs. But listen, the night you met George, Joanna and I had a visitor. Hannah, that girl who goes to the club came round.'

'I know who you mean. She's coming off drugs.'

'She's doing well. She said she couldn't believe it when she heard about my background. The kids all think you're so good, Stefan, they couldn't believe you'd married someone who'd . . .'

'Oh, Martha, you're the one who's good, not me.'

'No, but do you know what I mean? Hannah said it

gave her hope.'

'I see . . .' Stefan said slowly.

'Leo's made a big impression on them as well. A lot of the kids at the club have been up before the court. They know they did wrong, and they know that Leo only ever speaks the truth. They want to protect him, Hannah says. Some of the boys are going to take turns to be his bodyguard.'

'Oh no, Martha, they mustn't. That will just give the police another excuse to attack Leo.'

'What are you so alarmed about? You mustn't get a police what's it called, phobey – something – when you're scared of things.'

'Phobia, I think. No, but . . .' But Martha didn't know about the latest encounter with the police, and so Stefan said no more.

'It will help the boys stay out of trouble. If they're guarding Leo they won't go stealing things.'

'I suppose so. It will just be trouble of a different kind, though.'

'A better kind,' Martha argued. 'Anyway, Hannah said she'd like to come to church, so we went and lit a candle and Hannah asked me to teach her how to say a prayer. She said the church was full of peace and she'd go again on her own, but she'll come with us to the litany on Saturday too. Wouldn't Michael be pleased? Oh, Stefan, I was so looking forward to Christmas with us all. Niki didn't understand about Christmas last year, and we had the horrible news that you weren't getting home, as well as all our worries about Michael.'

'Do you know what Andrey, Thomas and I have been thinking? It was Thomas's idea, of course. We could try to phone.'

'Phone Michael? Do you think we really could? They'll listen to every word of course.'

'That's the problem. Andrey thinks it's too dangerous. We'd need to find some way of dialling direct. Thomas has a phone at home, but we don't want him to get his family into trouble. Elizabeth is leaving for another foreign tour this Christmas. Listen, we're invited out tonight. Joanna too. Andrey has asked us round to his room. He's going to cook a meal for us.'

'How nice!'

'I know. It seems there's a surprise waiting for us.'

The surprise was an envelope which was lying on the table in Andrey's cupboard-sized room in the parish house. He laid his fingers to his lips. 'Walls have ears. Just wait till videos get installed.'

'We'll be first in line for one,' said Martha but Andrey was handing them the envelope, and now they saw the initials S. and M. Corn.

'Carrier pigeon,' Andrey explained. 'A roundabout route. I tell you what, Joanna, I've got the salad dressing ready just to mix together. Come and tell me if I'm doing the right things. I'd be glad of your expert advice.'

'How tactful of him,' Martha said as Andrey shut the door. 'Open the envelope, please, Stefan, my hands are shaking too much.'

Stefan unfolded the paper. The well-known old-fashioned handwriting told them at once who the writers were, but just the same Stefan looked down at the signatures at the end: M. and H.

And underneath a scribble: 'Niki', and Helen's writing: 'his special message to his dear Martha.'

Dear friends whom we miss and pray for, the letter began. *Thank you for your gifts, which our friend here brought home to us. We are glad to hear that you are well and happy. We receive some of your letters – good that you number them, and we rejoice with you at your happy news, wishing we could be with you to help you and share in the birth when it comes, around Easter, you think? Our parting from you was so painful. There have been many sad partings, but only one other has ever been as hard as that farewell. Yet love crosses boundaries and cheers the saddest heart. Sometimes here, far from our homeland and our dear ones, we feel sad, but then joy returns and we know: someone is praying for us. We don't deserve your prayers but we need them for strength, missing home as we do, lecturing, discuss-*

ing, giving interviews and talks, sometimes to very few people, sometimes in crowded halls, and everything in a foreign language. Sometimes we are received with a measure of hostility and disbelief, but usually with great generosity and joy. We tell our new friends how you both brought light and joy to us and what you still endure. It is good news about the work in the crèche, as well as in the club. May you both experience Christ's peace in everything.

The path of faith is seldom easy. There is a different kind of hardship here: an emptiness which is hard for us to adapt to. The flame flickers faintly within a very great cold, whereas in Koravia many people, and you two in particular, have found that pearl of very great price, which is worth more than anything else in the world. We ourselves, this season of Advent, long for faith to be free in our homeland, but because we have sung the victory song while we were still in chains we know that it is not politics but love which sets people free. So we pray for you, and for all our friends whom we love and miss, especially your dear mother and our friends in K. Please greet them warmly from us and tell them we pray that the light of Christ will continue to shine in our homeland.

'Oh, Stefan, what a wonderful letter! It's just like having Michael in the room with us, you know his serious way of saying things and all the long words he uses . . . and then he smiles and there's just nothing on earth that's more cheer-up-making. Oh, Stefan, do you think we'll ever see them again?'

His hand reached out for hers. 'Let's be glad about the letter,' he said.

They read it through several times and shared it with their friends. After they had eaten, at Andrey's suggestion they copied the letter out several times. Soon copies were circulating throughout Koravia.

'So even though they're far away Michael and Helen and Niki are still part of our life. I'd rather have them living here though,' Martha added as she went on sewing the shirt she was making Niki. 'Here's a piece of news, though. Matusha is getting a phone installed. She told me that last time I went to see her.'

'I have news as well. They're giving me two days off at Christmas,' Stefan said, 'providing, of course I work New Year.'

'So things are working well.' said Martha, but her voice was sad. 'We had everything to look forward to last Christmas,' she sighed. 'I'm sorry, Stefan, I mustn't go on like this. We've got the baby, after all.'

'We've got each other,' Stefan said.

10

'The interests of our citizens'

'There's the Christmas star,' Martha pointed beyond bare, snow-covered limes to the frosty sky above Lipa's wooden houses. Her hand went to her side. 'The baby wants to see it too.'

Stefan put his arm round her. 'That star is shining for Michael and Helen and Niki in Ostrova.'

'I know. We must tell Matusha that the star is out. We can light the candles on the tree and start our meal now.'

They stood around the candle-lit tree. 'As we sing our carol let's remember our absent friends,' Maria said.

'And George,' Stefan added. 'Is he coming for New Year, Mother?'

'I don't know. I've tried phoning him. Now, you two sit down and I'll bring the soup. No, Martha, you're not to help. Tonight you are going to be a lady.'

Stefan pulled a chair out for Martha. 'You look gorgeous tonight,' he told her.

She caught his hand and pressed it to her cheek. 'How rough and hacked your hand is! Workworn. Yet you never complain.'

'I guess I'm not ambitious. That side of me changed when I met Michael. What's that?'

'The phone. Of course, you haven't heard it ringing in your mother's house before.'

'You answer it, Stefan,' his mother called from the kitchen, 'though I can't think who on earth can be phoning at this time. Perhaps it's George.'

'Lipa 660 . . . Hello. Sorry, I can't hear you . . . It's

from abroad.'

'*Abroad*?' Martha pushed back her chair and hurried over beside him.

'Dr Green . . . hello. Christmas greetings. Yes, it's Stefan. Martha's right beside me. She sends her greetings too. What's that? Michael wants to speak . . . oh, yes please. Michael! It's good to hear you. How clear you sound! Martha's snatching the phone from me. Here she is.'

'Michael, Michael, how did you guess, we're just sitting down to eat this minute. No, of course you haven't disturbed us. How's Niki? Is he all excited about Christmas? What's that – he wants to speak . . . Hello, Niki, It's Martha, are you being a good boy . . .? Hello, Helen. Christmas greetings! Yes, we're fine . . .'

'They're going to eat their Christmas meal later, because their time is behind ours,' Martha explained, handing the phone over to her mother-in-law. 'Our parcels arrived safely, and Niki is wearing the shirt I made – he looks a true Koravian, Helen says, just like you do, Stefan, in your embroidered shirt.

But Stefan was speaking now. 'Everything's fine. Joanna's passed her exams. What's that – an invitation . . . Sorry? Yes, I heard you this time: application forms, just for Martha and the baby. Dr Green is organising the tickets? Please thank her very much. I'll give you Martha again. No, we won't say "good-bye", only "see you" and "God bless". Yes, thank you, Michael, and we pray for you too . . .'

'What . . . an invitation?' Martha was whispering. She took the phone from Stefan. 'Michael, this is the best Christmas present ever! It's so good to hear you again, but what's all this I hear Stefan saying? An invitation for me to come and stay with Dr Green next summer? I can't believe it! You're telling us now so that we can start applying for visas. Oh, Michael, pray that they'll give us one. All by myself . . . well, with the baby, of course. Depends how things develop. Yes, I understand . . . God bless, Michael. God bless, Helen, thank you for the call. Hug Niki from me. God bless, Niki, darling. Have a lovely Christmas . . . Oh, Niki, Niki, I miss you so much. 'Bye, then, Michael . . . Christmas joy to you as well. 'Bye.'

The phone clicked the other end, but Martha still cradled the receiver in her hand. 'A phone call from Michael! And an invitation, but it can only be for me. *They* won't give permission for a husband and wife to travel, expecially a couple like us. It will all be done in Dr Green's name, but of course I'll be with Michael and Helen the whole time, the baby and me . . . Stefan, I can't believe it! Imagine, I've never been abroad before, or even in an aeroplane. That's not what matters of course, it's seeing Helen and Michael and Niki, but I'll hate going without you.'

'Well, that's something to look forward to,' Maria said, bringing in traditional clear soup and pastries. 'See how small the world has become. Your baby isn't born yet, but it's being invited to travel abroad already.'

'You'll be just like a pop star, jet-setting off on your foreign holiday,' teased Stefan later that evening as they joined groups of villagers all making their way to church.

'Oh, Stefan, I'll be missing you. Besides, it may not work out.'

'We'll pray that it will,' Stefan said.

'Thomas will load me up with all sorts of information for Dr Green. I don't mind, of course. That's important too, but the best thing is being with our friends. He doesn't think that way about things, though.'

But when Thomas came up to their flat on the evening of the second of January when they were all home from work, he was more agitated than they had ever known him.

'What is it, Thomas?' Stefan asked.

'It's Elizabeth . . .' he looked around the room.

'Do you want us to talk outside?' Stefan offered.

Snow whirled past their attic window, and coated Tarnov's domes with winter coverings.

'No, no, it's all right. the regime knows all about it anyway.'

'Knows all about what? Look, Thomas, I'll go and make some tea.'

'No, I'll go, Martha,' Stefan said.

'It's all right,' Thomas said. 'I'd rather you stayed to hear the news.' He rubbed his long fingers across his face. 'It's the first time we've had the police at the door, and Mother is so upset.'

Stefan and Martha looked at each other.

I was only fourteen when the police came for me, Stefan thought, but he pushed the thought away instantly, especially as Thomas had the humilty to add, 'I know it's nothing compared with what you've been through. Or Leo. He's tailed all the time these days. They keep their car parked outside the parish house. He sends them out hot tea, you know. Those boys from the club take it out to them.'

'And they talk about openness! But you still haven't told us what's happened to Elizabeth,' Stefan said.

'She's defected,' Thomas said.

'Defected!'

'Of course, she was on a tour at Christmas,' Martha recalled. 'Where is she, Thomas?'

'Ostrova.'

'That's where Michael and Helen are. That's all right then. They'll be able to help her.'

'Oh, Martha, it's not so simple. I mean, they're in the same city, Strandon, but it's got about eight million people.'

'I'm sure Elizabeth could find out their address.'

'Perhaps.'

'Cheer up, Thomas! We've never seen you as down as this,' Martha said. 'You're usually six steps ahead of the rest of us. Perhaps some good will come out of it for Elizabeth.'

'She'll never be allowed back to Koravia. You're an enemy if you try to leave our closed country.'

'Like Michael. He didn't even want to leave either.

They kicked him out,' Martha said. 'But contact abroad is easing. They can send invitations now. Dr Green is going to invite me.'

'Leave it, Martha. He's too upset to take it in. We'll tell you about it later, Thomas. But Martha's right. I'm sure Michael and Helen will do their best to contact Elizabeth once they know.'

'She may not want to have anything to do with them. Haven't you noticed that she's given up going to church and everything?'

'Do you know why she made her decision, Thomas?' Martha asked after a pause. 'After all, she had quite a good life here.'

'She had everything going for her. Mother thinks there was a man, someone she met on that tour last summer. She's been restless and upset ever since. So you see it has nothing to do with religious oppression or politics or anything.'

'Oh but it has,' Martha said quickly. 'Indirectly, anyway. If our border wasn't closed, Elizabeth wouldn't have to do anything so drastic.'

'Drastic, that's the right word for it. Drastic for us too.'

'Why, what are they doing to you? I'm sorry, Thomas, we should have asked you before,' Stefan apologised.

'They've chucked me out of my job,' Thomas said.

'Whatever for? I mean, you've been involved in all sorts of things they didn't like: the printing outfit, collecting information and giving "criminals" like Michael, Andrey and Stefan so much support,' Martha said, 'yet they never touched you.'

'Well, they've done it now. I've to work with a shovel stoking their fires,' Thomas said bitterly. 'It's the end of everything for me.'

'That's terrible,' Stefan began.

'That's typical,' Martha put in. 'You know it is, both of you.'

Her brisk remark annoyed Thomas. 'Oh yes, we know. If it had been for a real reason I might have accepted it – for helping someone like Michael, for instance, or because I take an active part in the church, but no. My sister, who was given all the chances, has a sordid love affair with some foreigner and we all have to suffer.'

'I think I will go and make that tea,' Stefan said.

'Listen, Thomas, I'm sorry you're having all this hassle,' Martha said, 'but Elizabeth is entitled to live her own life. She doesn't have to, oh dear, what is the word I want, confirm – no that's not it: never mind. What I'm trying to say is that you're trying to make Elizabeth fit into a mould, a good Koravian Christian girl. You can't stop people falling in love, even if it's with what you and your mother think are the wrong types.'

'You're the expert, of course, Martha,' Thomas replied icily. 'We all know what types you used to mix with.'

'What types Martha mixed with – what's all this about?' asked Stefan, coming back into the room with the tea things.

'Oh, forget it,' Thomas returned. 'I shouldn't have dragged it up. I'm upset, that's all, and Martha preaching at me didn't help.'

'I wasn't preaching,' Martha said, 'but I'm not going to quarrel, Thomas, so let's just forget it.'

'That was generous of you,' Stefan said, when Thomas had gone. 'It's upsetting for him, losing his job, of course,' he added.

'Losing it because of a love affair,' Martha reminded her husband. 'Oh, I'm sorry, let's stop talking about Thomas. I suppose he can't help the way he is. I wonder if George turned up in the end. When we phoned Matusha from that call box on New Year's evening there was no sign of him.'

'Perhaps I'll call round at his flat after work tomorrow,' Stefan said, but that night repeated ringing of the doorbell shrilled through all three floors of their house and got everyone up.

'Stefan Cornelius?' Two uniformed policemen stood

on the doorstep.

Icy air swirled in from the street. Martha trembled.

'Please come in and shut the door,' Stefan said. 'We live on the top floor.'

'No need to go upstairs.' Their voices boomed throught the building.

'It would be more private,' Martha suggested.

'We can say what we need to here,' one of the officers told her, while the other held an unintelligible dialogue with a walkie-talkie.

'Are you brother to George Antony Cornelius, house 12, room 22, Victory Square?'

'Yes.'

'George Cornelius is in the emergency wing of Tarnov State Hospital.'

'In hospital? What's happened?'

'He attempted to take his own life while under arrest in Tarnov State Prison.'

'Under arrest? What for?'

'We can't divulge such information.'

'When was he arrested?'

One of the officers sheafed through his papers. 'He was taken into custody at 4 a.m. on New Year's Day.'

'So that's way he didn't turn up at home. But why wasn't my mother told?'

'A slip-up owing to pressure of work over the holdiay period, no doubt. Deeply regretted.'

'I'm sure it is,' put in Martha. 'Does Mrs Cornelius know that her son is in hospital?'

'A police car was despatched to her village to take her to his bedside.'

'That's very kind of the police,' said Stefan. 'Thank you very much.'

'Not at all. The police always have the interests of our citizens at heart.'

Stefan and Martha exchanged glances. 'Well, er, yes.'

'If you want to go and visit your brother now we shall escort you by car.'

Another look passed between Stefan and Martha. 'May

I come too?' Martha asked.

'Only next of kin allowed,' one of the policemen boomed. 'Besides, in your condition, Citizenness, it would not be advisable. Upsetting, you know.'

'I'm kind of upset already,' Martha said.

'Quite, quite. All the more reason. We shall wait for you in the car then, Comrade Cornelius.' They marched to the door.

'Oh, Stefan, what's happening now? Is it a trick?'

'I don't think so. If they had wanted to arrest me I'd have been manhandled out to that car by now.'

'I suppose so. You'd better get ready but I don't like this at all. I felt the baby turn right over when they asked for you. Oh, those booming voices!' Martha went on breathlessly as they reached the last flight of stairs. "The police always have the interests of our citizens at heart". Since when, I wonder? Can we trust them, do you think?'

'I wish I knew. Poor George, if it is all true. He's reached the bottom now by his way of thinking at any rate.'

'Poor Matusha. Poor us. Stefan, don't go. Wait till the morning. If only we had a phone. We could contact the hospital and see if George really is there. I'm telling you, I won't be able to sleep. Imagine if they take you right away.' She peered out of the window. 'They're still there. I can't see how many of them there are. Listen. I'll put on my coat and see you out to the car.'

'What good will that do? No, I know what we'll do. I'll make my own way there. It's not far to the hospital. Does that make you feel happier?'

'So long as they don't follow you.'

'If I'm followed I'll come back here – by a roundabout route, of course. I know Tarnov well enough now.'

'All right then, Stefan. God bless you, my dear husband. Give Matusha my love, won't you? She must come back here for as long as she needs to be in Tarnov. I'll watch from the window.'

Three minutes later the police car drove away without

Stefan. Martha saw his slight figure in its shabby coat wave from the corner. She waved back and stood at the window for a long time until the thought of work the next day drove her back into bed.

Stefan had work to go to as well, but he sat beside his mother and a prison warder amidst a network of tubes and bottles at George's bed.

'He cut his wrists,' Maria said. 'I thought you'd never come.'

'I'm sorry, Mother, but Martha couldn't bear to see me disappearing in a police car. Do you know what he was arrested for?'

'Does it matter? Drunk and disorderly, I think. He has made powerful enemies, Stefan, and they're getting back at him now.'

'I guess so, but it's bad for you too. You've been through too much.'

'Too much,' Maria sighed, but her face softened at those words.

Stefan touched her hand. 'I'm truly sorry for my share in your troubles. You've always stood by me, and I appreciate that more than I can say.'

She nodded. 'That's nice to hear . . . Poor George! He had such a splendid future ahead. I'm glad your father isn't alive to see him now.'

'I think you should to home to bed, Mother. Martha says you must stay with us for as long as you like.'

'We'll have to see how George gets on.'

Next day Stefan and Maria arrived back at the hospital to find that George had surfaced into consciousness. He recognized them, but instead of greeting them he closed his eyes and turned his head away.

'George,' his mother said. 'Can you hear me?'

But George made no attempt to reply.

'It's hopeless. He's depressed, needing alchohol too, I guess,' Stefan told Martha that night. 'And of course they'll transfer him back to prison and we'll be lucky if we get a chance to visit him then.'

Stefan went back to see George after work next day. His mother was beside the bed as usual.

'He seems a bit better today,' she whispered to Stefan. 'They've taken all those tubes away, but he still isn't speaking.'

Stefan leant over his brother. 'George, they'll move you soon. Please talk to us. Say something, George. The police brought Mother here two nights ago.'

George turned his head. His mouth was furred. Stefan held a glass of water to his lips. George took a sip, but when he spoke his voice was bitter. 'Another delinquent in the Cornelius family.'

'No, George, it's not like that,' Stefan said. 'You're sick. You need treatment.'

'Listen to the great expert! So that's your diagnosis, is it, Dr Cornelius. I'm sick, am I?'

'Don't, George,' his mother began, and Stefan tried to explain, 'You need help to stop you drinking, George.'

'Who says I'm drunk? Or have you got some inside knowledge from the court?'

'Of course, I haven't.'

'Well, then . . .'

'Have you got a court case coming up then, George?' his mother asked.

'Oh, no, Mother, they're just keeping me in prison out of the goodness of their hearts.'

Stefan and his mother exchanged glances.

'There's nothing more we can say,' his mother sighed. 'We're all the family you've got, George. We've sat beside you day and night and all you can do is insult us.'

'What do you expect?' he returned. 'Or do you want me to grovel?'

'Sit up, George,' ordered Stefan.

'What's all this?'

'I haven't been a nurse for nothing.' Stefan told him, launching an attack on George's flopping pillows. He fetched warm water and a scrap of carbolic soap which someone had overlooked and sponged his brother's hands and face, straightened the sheets, positioned him comfortably, and poured fresh drinking water. All the time there was a picture in his mind of George, an army officer, standing above him with whips and commands to hurt and arrest.

He wanted to hurt me. It was all set up just for that, George's revenge on me. It cost Michael his freedom. George planned it all. But he couldn't hurt me. He only hurt himself.

'I'm going home now, George. We probably won't see you again, but I'll be in court the day of your trial.'

'No way – I don't want you there,' growled George.

11

'Victims become victors'

'So you see the set-up, Stefan,' Thomas pushed open a heavy fire door which led into a corridor in the gas works. 'I sleep here,' he indicated a couch covered with a grimy cloth. 'I have my own table, but best of all, no one inspects us. They don't bother about people as low as the workers here.'

'Bottom of the ladder, Thomas!' teased Stefan, 'It has its advantages. I like your artwork.'

The brick wall in the corner of the gas works where Thomas did night shift was decorated with hand-written cards. There was a colour poster of the Koravian Highlands and photographs of Helen and Michael, Brother Leo, Holy Cross Church; even, Stefan was touched to see, a wedding photograph of him and Martha.

' "There comes a time when fear, like mist over mountains, lifts to reveal sunlit places".' Stefan read aloud words which Thomas had printed on a card. They came from a prison letter written by Nikolai, the friend who had given his orange and his dwindling strength to Stefan eight years before in labour camp.

'That's true, about fear lifting,' Thomas said. 'Have some tea.' He poured strong brew into the bottom of two glasses and topped it up with hot water from an ancient kettle. 'It's happened to me: since I've been here all the black feelings I had have disappeared. Here.' He handed Stefan tea.

'Thanks.'

'I want you to tell Martha that I'm sorry for what I said that time.'

'That's all right, Thomas.'

'No, it isn't. I've thought about it a lot, working here at night. I always imagined I'd seen through the system.'

'So you did,' Stefan told him warmly. 'Remember how you spoke to me when you were doing that wiring job in the hospital? People on the make never bother to talk to anyone as menial as a junior nurse.'

'Thanks, Stefan, but that's not entirely true. I'd heard about you from my sister, remember. I knew you'd been in prison. I wanted to meet people who knew where it was at.'

'You're doing yourself down, Thomas. You risked a lot when we were all involved with printing, and you kept in touch with Michael and me when we were in prison.'

'Maybe so, but I was still cushioned. Being here has taught me a lot. Some of the guys would nick the sugar out of your tea, but they've all seen through the system. They think a whole lot of Leo, by the way. Others are here because they're considered too ideologically dangerous to be put anywhere else, except prison of course. One of them is a leading mathematician, an algebra specialist, Dr Volski. There's quite a lot of activity going on, a study group, for instance. In fact, stoking is a good name for what we do here. We're a melting pot for information and there are no bugging devices or anything.'

'Ask that maths expert if he's mended his sock yet . . . It sounds like you don't mind being here, after all.'

'It was hard at first,' Thomas admitted. 'After all, I was a senior electrician, not far from being a master. But what do these sort of titles mean? You're right, Stefan, being at the bottom has its advantages. It's the only place in our society where a man can feel really free.'

'A woman too,' Stefan reminded him. 'They're the ones in touch with the things which really matter. I learnt that from Helen long ago.'

'Martha's like that as well,' Thomas said, generously. 'I'm sure that's why the kids in the club like her so much. Andrey tells me about it. I've been, out of a sense of duty, I guess, and kind of wanting to be where it's happening, like I say, but I could never mix.'

'You seem to be doing all right here. It sounds as though there's plenty going on.'

'You're right on both counts. I don't feel so sore about Elizabeth, either. Mother misses her, of course, and it's terrible to think we may never see her again, but as Martha says, things are easing. I felt jealous that Dr Green had invited Martha – well, it's Helen and Michael really.'

'Jealous?'

'You wouldn't understand that, would you? That's the first thing I noticed about you. There's no self-seeking in you, Stefan.'

'Oh, I don't know, but don't let's get into all that. I'm glad things are working out. Martha and I were worried about you. Why don't you come round and see us? Martha stops work at the end of this month.'

'Okay, I will. You will tell her what I said, though.'

'Of course. Don't think about it any more.'

Just the same when Thomas next came to see them he had a box of chocolates for Martha.

'Chocolates! You just want to make me fatter than ever!' exclaimed Martha, but they all knew what Thomas's present was meant to say.

'Not long till I'm a lady of leisure,' Martha went on, curling up on the couch with her sewing.

'How long will you get for maternity leave?'

'A whole six months. Isn't it bliss?'

'But no one gets that amount of maternity leave!'

'I know, and I'll be asking for the month of October off too. That's when we've decided my foreign trip will be. We've applied already. It's just like being one of *them*! Wives of high up Party officials get maternity leave – well, lots of them don't even work, and have chances for foreign travel.'

'So how are you managing it" Thomas asked.

'Oh, my husband's influence,' Martha said airily.

'He's so highly placed, you know. No, what really happened is that Hannah, one of the girls from the club, is going to take over my job. I won't get any pay, of course, but I won't get thrown out, either. We're both hoping it will lead to her getting a job in the crèche afterwards, which will be good. The doctor is pleased with me too,' Martha added. 'Our little baby is doing everything a baby should, like waking its daddy up at nights with all its kicking!'

'Can you really feel it kicking?' Thomas asked, and they had to laugh at his astonishment.

'The other thing is that our house has got a phone now. We all share it. Matusha phoned, Stefan. George's trial has been fixed for next week and she's wondering if you'll be able to get off work to go.'

'Of course. I'll just have to change my shifts.'

'It will be a new thing for you to be in a courtroom as part of the public and not on show,' Martha pointed out.

Stefan remembered her words as he sat in the public gallery waiting for George's turn to be tried. He had a medical book open in front of him, but it was hard to concentrate.

I was lucky. I always knew that someone cared about me: Mother and Sister Helen, that first time; and Michael when I was up before the military tribunal. Michael was with me at my other trial too.

A broken, beaten man who had bent his head to the floor in desperate prayer.

I wonder if George will notice me. He makes out that he doesn't even care. Let something happen today to help George, please, Lord Jesus. Don't let him be sent to prison. He needs to know he's not the complete failure he thinks he is.

Failure – perhaps, as Nik knew, it's the place where hope begins. Thomas has found that out, anyway.

The judge and the procurator appeared and the hearing began. George stood between prison warders to hear his charge. Drunk and disorderly.

'You were a distinguished army officer and now you brawl in the gutter like a hooligan,' the judge reprimanded the prisoner in her summing up. 'I was going to send you to prison.'

Stefan craned forward. Prison, no – *was going*, but the judge was still speaking. 'Instead I shall fine you four thousand crowns. You will be employed from now on as a labourer, building the new extension to the geriatric hospital.'

Four thousand crowns! That was stiff. If George defaulted they would send him to prison. Stefan hurried outside to try to catch his brother, but George looked through him.

'George, it's me, Stefan.'

'Come to gloat, have you? Comrade Captain George Cornelius has become a labourer.'

'There are worse things to be.'

'Look who's talking. Don't kid yourself. I may be at the bottom, but I still choose my company. I'd have to be even lower than I am just now to want anything to do with you.'

Stefan bit his lip. His brother's face was hard with hatred.

Was it always like this? Images from childhood flashed through Stefan's mind. George telling his younger brother to ignore Sister Helen and the children's club she organised. George arguing with their grandmother, trying to make her conform with the new regime. Earlier memories too, of himself pulling his mother down to whisper childish secrets he sensed his elder brother would mock.

'Can't you get it into your thick head that I don't want anything to do with you?'

But that wasn't true, was it? *Was it?*

As if in answer, like the replay of an old film, a picture of Michael flashed into Stefan's mind – Michael as he had first known him, starved, unwashed, cold, rising to his feet submissively as the boys who were to torment him, Stefan and his fellow soldier, marched into his cell. A light had flashed into his eyes, a flicker, almost a question, and those eyes had been Stefan's undoing.

I understood that question. Were we really thugs? That's what he was asking. So I couldn't carry out those orders. I attacked him, but I'd already weakened. He knew it too. I'll never forget the way he touched my shoulder. 'You're too young for a hell like this,' he said. He knew I was as much a victim as him. More, even. And that's what pulled me out of the pit. And so I know now that George doesn't mean a word he says. But how can I show him?

Stefan swallowed hard. 'It's not true what you say about not wanting to know me. I've got to go to work now, but I want to come and see you.'

George's mouth formed an answer, but no words came. He swung round and marched away. Stefan hesitated and set off in the opposite direction. His brother's retreating footsteps rang in his ears. The sound, harsh with contempt, still sounded inside his head as he scraped greasy pots.

He's hurt, so he's got to hit back, he told me so himself, he thought.

'Orderly Cornelius! Charge nurse wants you. Better hurry, she doesn't like to be kept waiting.'

Stefan hurried down the ward towards the office.

The charge nurse looked up from her desk.

'Orderly, I see you've applied for nursing studies.'

'Yes, Comrade Nurse. I passed second year physiology last autumn.'

'Is that so? You've kept on with your studies? I must say I get excellent reports about you from staff and patients. It's really only your religious beliefs which made you, shall we say, somewhat suspect?'

Was it still the same old story?

'However, things are changing in our society. Believers like you can contribute to the life of our nation in a most positive way, and I must say, Cornelius, that all the reports I have here indicate that you show a quality which is quite remarkable. Tell me, would you consider that the caring, honest attitude you show is a direct result of your religious beliefs?'

'She said it so seriously,' Stefan told Martha afterwards. 'I couldn't believe it.'

'*Caring, honest attitude* – that's something different from the things they used to say about people like us. Whatever did you answer?'

'I didn't know what to say,' Stefan replied. 'I just said, "well, er, yes".'

'Or something equally breath-taking,' Martha teased.

'You could say so. Anyway, I've to start nursing training after Easter. They're letting me into the second year course, providing I pass a medical procedures exam in March.'

'Oh, Stefan, that is good news! So you'll be a father and a nurse together.'

'And you'll be a mother.'

'It feels very like it,' Martha replied. 'It's odd, though, the things they're saying now about belief. Sometimes it looks as though it's acceptable and open, and other times, like Michael's letters never arriving, it's as dark and difficult as ever. Our little baby is going to be born into a confused sort of country.'

'Telephone for Cornelius.'

'Who can it be at this time of night? It's almost midnight.'

'I'll go and see.' Stefan hurried down three flights of stairs and picked up the phone.

'Stefan, it's Andrey speaking. Listen, there's terrible news. I don't know how to tell you. It's Leo. He's been murdered.'

'Wh–at?'

The phone crackled and went dead. 'Hello, hello.' No reply. He put the receiver down. What was Andrey's number, now? It was in his notebook upstairs. Was there any point trying to phone back? He hurried upstairs on legs which shook beneath him.

'It was Andrey,' he told Martha, 'but the line went

dead. It seemed urgent. I'm going round to talk to him.'

'At this time of night? It must be an emergency.'

'I'm sorry, love, but yes, it is.' He kissed Martha. 'Go to bed, dearest. I'll come in as quietly as I can.'

He was trembling as he went outside into the February night. Murdered. Leo, the gentle parish worker who preached forgiveness. What was it Martha had heard him say, 'Love turns hardship to glory.' And now . . . Oh yes, it was all too likely. 'They have their methods'. It wasn't so long ago they'd broken both his legs. What had happened this time? Another car crash?

The parish house was a hive of activity. Press men pushed microphones and recording machines at reluctant clergy. Cameras flashed. Boys with police records had their arms round Leo's sobbing relatives. A crowd was beginning to gather. Stefan pushed through.

'Andrey? The phone went dead on us. Thomas? You've heard about it too. What's happened? What did they do?'

There hadn't been a car crash. Bit by bit he sorted out the story. Leo had gone on a preaching tour of eastern Koravia, taking with him his litany for the home-land as well as some of the boys and girls from the club – and of course *they* had followed him too, Andrey added grimly.

'He wasn't at supper, this evening, but that's nothing unusual, so no one felt worried. But then he didn't turn up for the litany – the very thing he'd come for. The church was packed, of course. People waited and still he didn't come. So they went to look for him.'

Two boys from the club, together with a group of men from the remote mountain village where the service was to take place had found Leo's body, beaten and mangled, hanging from a tree.

'Hanged – with his hands tied behind his back,' Andrey said.

Tense and upset, Stefan listened to facts which were about to be repeated in news reports all over the world.

Popular preacher murdered by security police.

Thousands attend church of murdered preacher.
Hanged preacher opens closed border.
Whole world flocks to Koravia.

Leo's murder affected everyone. Even George wanted to talk about it.

'He visited me in prison. There was something about that guy – and I'm stone sober, I promise,' he added. 'A flame,' he went on, 'that's it. So they've snuffed his light for ever.'

'People are saying the light is only beginning,' said Stefan.

'Could be,' George replied seriously. 'For years they've been saying that guys like him – and you, I've got to say, were criminals. Now they're declaring themselves the murderers. I wouldn't like to be the man who tied that noose. The regime is going to need scapegoats. They're already talking about putting the police on trial. It makes me glad I'm well out of their power games.'

I'm glad too, Stefan thought. Conversations like these built bridges between them. And similar discussions were heard everywhere.

'Everyone in Koravia seems to be a believer nowadays,' Martha remarked.

Leo's murder brought the whole world to Koravia.

In a well advertised amnesty it even brought Helen and Michael on a four-week visa.

'And Niki! Oh, Niki!' Martha bent her swollen body towards the little boy. 'How you've grown.'

'I flew here with Mummy and Daddy,' said Niki solemnly.

'Listen to the grown up way he talks! Andrey is putting you up in the parish house – just think, in the very same bed where we slept after they sent you away. But isn't it terrible about Leo? He thought so much of you, Michael. You must come and see our room. It's high among the rooftops, Niki, up lots of stairs. We're just like little birds in a nest. I'm sure you've got a room of your own. I've seen pictures of your house. It looks enormous.'

Martha's mood, a mixture of elation and sorrow, was felt by everyone in the heady yet horrific days which preceded Leo's funeral in Holy Cross Church.

The world's media summarised and analysed events.

Ferment of religious fervour spreads through Koravia
Police state opens its criminal records
Victims become victors as tension mounts in Koravia

'Everyone's an expert on Koravia nowadays,' Martha commented. 'Some foreign broadcasts are even forecasting the overthrow of the police state, Helen says. Oh, Stefan, isn't it good to have them with us again! A whole month, and now I'm off work I can spend every day with them, but I can see that Michael isn't very well, and Helen had a miscarriage last month. It was her sixteenth week. Isn't it nice to think a couple as old as them still makes love. Do you think we'll enjoy lovemaking when we're forty plus like them?'

'You'll be as gorgeous then as you are now,' Stefan assured her.

'What are we thinking of, Stefan? We shouldn't be talking like this when . . . oh it's too horrible for words. Leo's parents had to identify his body. Have you seen the photographs?'

'Yes, they're grim. Like George said, I wouldn't like to be the men who did the murder.'

'Or be married to them. Imagine!'

'We must pray for them,' Stefan said seriously. 'There's a vigil all week in Holy Cross Church with special prayers for Leo's killers.'

No one slept. No one went to work. The only trams which were full were the ones which went to Holy Cross Church. Intellectuals mingled with factory workers and clergy. Thin faced women whom everyone knew were secret nuns brought sick and disabled adults and children, who were never otherwise seen in public, to pray beside Leo's coffin. Other handicapped people dragged themselves there on crutches, or were helped along by friends. A new headline was blazoned across newspapers in countries outside Koravia:

Murdered preacher becomes police state's patron saint.

Men rolled up their trouser legs and walked on their knees along the pavements outside Holy Cross Church. Suddenly every kiosk sold candles along with newspapers and bus tickets. You couldn't buy a flower in Tarnov even at black market prices, yet still people came with armfuls of flowers, wreaths and garlands and messages which read, 'Leo, we love you. Freedom for Koravia. We pray for our homeland.'

Helen and Martha took Niki to church. 'We want to go and pray, Niki, because a good man was murdered.'

'What's "murdered"?' asked Niki.

'It's a very bad thing, Niki. Hold your candle nice and steady now and we'll pray together.'

'Niki can say "Our Father",' Helen said, and the little boy's voice piped the prayer beside the flowers and candles which covered the coffin. 'Forgive us our sins . . . as we forgive others . . .' Old women listening wept. Close behind them a child asked, 'Who was murdered? Was a good man murdered?'

'So even the youngest children learn that crime is part of our country's story,' Michael said as they sat together in Martha's and Stefan's room. 'In Ostrova they worry because small children watch violence on television. Our children experience murder too, but they also learn to pray for forgiveness.'

Leo was buried during a heavy snowfall with as many mourners as there were snowflakes. Afterwards, all day and night, patient, endless queues of people filed past the grave. Others, including Martha, Helen and Niki watched the funeral on television.

'Imagine, they're actually going to broadcast some of the service,' Martha told Stefan before the funeral. 'Thomas has invited us round. His mother has a television set. Did you know that Helen went to one of Elizabeth's concerts and had her back for a meal?'

'That's good news. How was Elizabeth?'

'Not very happy, I think. Things aren't going well with that man she met, but I don't think Helen wanted to say too much to worry Thomas.'

When the funeral was over the Laskis and Martha went to Lipa to see their friends. Maria hadn't come for the funeral. 'It's not her thing,' Martha said to Stefan, 'and Adam isn't able to cope with all the crowds. I wish you could come with us, Stefan.'

'I know, but I'll have to go back to work. I must study too. That exam is next week.'

'It's important that you pass, as well, Oh, but I wish this baby would come!'

Martha said the same thing as they sat in the kitchen in Stefan's old house in Lipa.

'It's such a drag now,' she complained.

'When is your date?' Helen asked.

'April the sixth,' Martha replied. 'Easter Day. But I hope I don't have to wait that long. Besides I want it to be born before you go home, so that you can see it too. We want you and Michael to be godparents.'

'We'll be very pleased,' Helen said, 'but I think you should just have one of us. Your baby needs godparents in Koravia too.'

'I expect you're right. Oh, but I do so wish I could have it now!'

'It will come when it's ready,' Helen assured her, 'like a leaf falling off the tree, although, alas, not quite so easily!'

The evening of their departure from Koravia Michael and Helen went for a last time to Leo's grave. Martha, Stefan and Niki came too.

They stood in silence beside the grave. It was five o'clock. Koravia had just changed its clocks to summer time. The sun was strong with the promise of spring, although snow still shrouded the churchyard and a cold wind put out the candles which were lit constantly around the grave. There was a continual stream of people. Many brought flowers. Some just stood and looked; others prayed. Despite the bitter wind men removed head coverings. A workman, obviously come straight from a building job, bent and lit a candle. Stefan looked across in his direction. It was George. Their eyes met. George nodded briefly and turned away.

There was something about that guy . . . a flame . . . they've snuffed his light for ever . . .

No, George, no, the light is still burning.

Then it was time to go to the airport for their farewell. 'Not goodbye,' said Helen firmly. 'We're seeing Martha in the autumn, with our little godchild too, we pray.'

'Who knows what further changes Leo's death will bring to Koravia?' added Michael. 'Resurrection hope comes out of darkness.'

Their flight was being called. 'Give our love to Dr Green,' said Stefan.

'We will. She'll have been sitting glued to her television, following the news of her beloved Koravia,' Helen said. 'Thank you both once again for all your letters and parcels. They mean so much to us.'

Michael made the sign of the cross over them. 'God bless you both, and the little one so soon to be born.'

Then the Laskis were caught up in queues pressing forward for their flight. A last wave from Michael, a last kiss blown to Niki, and Martha and Stefan were left alone.

'It's only until October,' Martha said. 'I can bear it this time, Stefan. Oh, but wasn't it lovely to see them again; and wasn't it good to see George at the grave?'

12

Rianna – first light of dawn

'Lipa 660.'

'Hello, Mother. It's Stefan. Martha's labour has started. I'm phoning from hospital now.'

'When did it begin?'

'Twelve hours ago, but the pains were slow at first.'

'How is she?'

'She's all right so far. They won't let me in until the baby's born.'

'Of course not. Men have no place in the maternity ward.'

I don't know, Stefan thought. I was in at the beginning, after all . . .

'I'll get a train straight away.'

'Okay . . . I'll see you later, then,'

He put the receiver down. Where now? His thoughts were all with Martha. I hated leaving her alone with total strangers. I hope she's all right. I hope the pains aren't too bad.

He paced up and down the corridor.

Was his mother right? Should men be excluded from childbirth? Helen said that in Ostrova things were often arranged so that couples could be together at the birth of their baby. But how could he begin to make those kind of comparisons? In Koravia the delivery of babies was considered unproductive. The job was left to over-worked midwives and doctors who couldn't make it in other branches of medicine.

Let Martha be all right.

She'd had a huge upsurge of energy yesterday morning

and had cleaned their room from top to bottom. Then she'd painted Easter eggs and prepared some of the traditional dishes.

'Joanna's gone home for the holidays,' she'd said. 'I must get everything ready.'

Church bells rang from Tarnov's towers. The Easter vigil was beginning. Each church contained a representation of Christ's grave. Men and boys mounted guard in shifts from Friday evening until dawn on Sunday.

We rise at deep dawn to welcome our joy.

The old words echoed in Stefan's thoughts. He was keeping a different kind of vigil tonight. Two years ago he'd been in labour camp with Andrey. Last year he and Martha had been planning their wedding, and praying for Michael, little knowing that he was being driven in a darkened car through the homeland which would soon deport him.

Women sought you in vain with myrrh and with tears. But an angel shone like a flame before day.

Stefan's restless feet took him past Holy Cross Church where Leo's grave was covered with spring flowers, palm branches, candles. Last year he had still been alive, preaching openly about Michael's unjust prison sentence, organising medical books for Stefan, getting his club started and visiting people in prison. People like George.

We've only met once since that time at the grave. Neither of us mentioned it, of course. He's staying off drink, but he still won't come to see us. I wonder if he'll bother once the baby is born?

The baby . . . Martha. He looked at his watch. Not even an hour since he had left her outside the ward. Could he phone yet? He had to go on duty tomorrow morning. Stefan Cornelius, second year nurse. What a training the last seven years had given him! First he had spent eight months locked up with grown men in a cramped prison cell awaiting trial for his crime of pulling down a party flag. Then he had served nine months on a building site, which was really a prison camp, where he had met the lifer, Nik, who had given him so much more than just the taste of sunlight and strength from an orange. Then, trapped by orders which he dared not disobey, and promises of a good life, which he wanted more than anything else, Stefan had won promotion in the army which put him back in prison camp, but on the other side this time; and there he had met Michael Laski, Nik's friend, Helen's long lost fiancé, the man Stefan had been ordered to 'rehabilitate'.

But I couldn't; I couldn't.

How can you beat a man who refuses to defend himself? Especially when more and more you're beginning to know that, however costly it is, the way Michael, Nik and Helen lived was the way he was beginning to believe in too, even if it took him right to the bottom of society: a medical orderly in a prison camp, a junior nurse, and then back to labour camp . . .

His thoughts whirled back to the present. Should he go and meet his mother from the train? It was too soon for that as well. He stopped at the next call-box and dialled the hospital number.

'Your wife is doing fine. Phone back later,' was all they would say.

He went home to try to cook a meal for Martha. Hospital food was so bad she would appreciate something extra. Cooking wasn't one of the skills which labour camp taught its inmates. Stefan had learnt more about going without food than getting it ready. Still he would try, and then perhaps he could phone the hospital again.

'Stefan, what on earth's happening here? I could smell burning all the way up the street, and when I opened your front door I thought the house must be on fire.'

'Well, the butter was hard, so I put it under the grill,' Stefan explained. 'I was trying to make a cheesecake for Martha, but all I've made is a mess.'

'You can say that again! Make me a pot of tea instead and I'll clean this lot up for you. It didn't occur to you I'd be bringing food from home, did it?'

'I didn't think . . .' he admitted.

'You're too strung up, that's the problem. Don't worry, Stefan. Women have been producing babies since the world began. Martha is young and strong. She'll be all right.'

If that was supposed to be comfort, it didn't help much, he reflected as he paced the hall floor where the telephone stood, lifted the receiver and dialled.

'Mrs Cornelius is doing fine. Call back later.'

'No news then?'

He shook his head.

I've been through some bad times but these are the worst hours of my life, he thought.

Almost as though she had guessed his thoughts his mother said, 'Really, Stefan, try to pull yourself together! After all you've had to cope with I should have thought you'd know how to keep calm in a crisis. It isn't even a crisis, either, as I keep telling you. It's the most natural thing in the world. Now, where do you keep the tea, because that kettle is almost boiling.'

'Just hot water for me, Mother.'

'Oh, Stefan, is that wise?'

'I might take some food tomorrow.'

'I think you should have something now. It will stop you feeling so jittery.'

He put down his glass. 'I think I'll go back to the hospital. I'm sorry to leave you with all this mess. I'll phone if I get any news.'

He paced the corridors and finally sat on a bench outside the ward and waited. Towards midnight a nurse put her head round the door.

'Stefan Cornelius?'

He leapt to his feet, 'Yes, yes, that's me.'

'Your wife's just had a lovely little girl.'

'Is she all right?'

'They're both doing fine.'

'Can I come and see her?'

'It's strictly against the rules. Come tomorrow. Visiting is from three till four in the afternoons, six till eight at night.'

'But I'm doing a spilt shift tomorrow. I'm a second year nurse. *Please,*' he added.

'A nurse?'

'Yes, in Tarnov State Hospital. I'll put on a mask and a gown, if you give me one.'

'A mask and a gown? And who'd wash them afterwards?'

So conditions in the maternity hospital were as bad as everyone said. Well, if they could break the rules of hygiene, surely the nurse could bend the regulations just a bit? Almost like an echo of his thoughts, the nurse said, 'Since you're a student nurse you can come in, but only for five minutes. If charge nurse comes along you'd better pretend to be a student of midwifery.'

'I'll say I got permission from one of my colleagues. Thank you more than I can possibly say.' He followed the nurse into the post-delivery room just as Martha's bed was wheeled into the overcrowded ward.

'Stefan!' Her face lit up. 'You know we've got a little girl?' she said as he bent and kissed her.

'Yes, the nurse told me.'

'Are you pleased?'

'Of course I am, darling!' His hand reached for hers. 'I wish I could see her. Where is she?'

'They put her in the nursery. I'll get her beside me tomorrow. I'm supposed to be getting some rest.'

'Oh, Martha, it's lovely to be with you, but I'm feeling guilty about it now. You look shattered.'

'No wonder! I've never worked so hard in my life! It's not called labour for nothing, you know. I managed it all on my own without any drugs or anything.'

'It was all right, then?'

'It wasn't a picnic. The hardest part is when you want to push but you mustn't. That's awful, Stefan, you feel as if you're being torn apart. I thought I'd die, but it's amazing how you forget once you actually hold the baby. She's sweet.'

'Like her mother . . .'

'No, I want to talk about her.'

'Mrs Cornelius, it's time you got some sleep.'

'I'll try to come in tomorrow, love. Mother's here. She'll be delighted at the news. God bless, sweetheart. Sleep well.'

'Oh, I will. Stefan, listen, her name's Rianna, right? I knew it as soon as they told me I was having a little girl, before she was properly through. Remember we said we might choose a Koravian name? Well, we have. And Joanna will be the other godmother.'

Rianna. It was an old word for the first light of dawn, for the morning star; the first rays of the sun: yes it was a good name for an Easter baby, born in the dark hours of the vigil, before the full light of day.

'Rianna. Are you sure? Well, these old Koravian names seem to be coming back into fashion nowadays,' his mother said. 'In our day we used Bible names or saints' names, like you both have. Anyway, I'm glad you got in to see Martha, and I'm sure you'll make your daughter's acquaintance soon enough. May I go in and see them both tomorrow?'

'Of course, and if you get to the hospital ahead of me you'll meet your granddaughter before her own father has set eyes on her.'

'That's a grandmother's privilege. In the old days grandmothers were present at the birth. A grandmother, my goodness! But look at you, yawning your head off, and no wonder! Get away to bed. You've got your work to go to in the morning.'

Stefan set his alarm for five. Trying not to disturb his mother, he pulled on his clothes and went outside. One or two people were already out and about. Windows were lit up. He imagined sleepy people washing, having breakfast. Some, like him, were heading for church to share the vigil before starting work. He knelt beside the model of Christ's grave. Silent watchers stood at each corner. One of them was Andrey, whose four hour shift would end at six am.

The church was cold and full of shadows.

Resurrection hope comes out of darkness.

Was Andrey remembering the stub of candle, the New Testament held against the beams from lights around the perimeter fence? He said so little about himself, always. Stefan knew that his dream was to enter seminary and train for work with the church; but such a dream was an impossibility for someone who had already fallen foul of the regime, as impossible as it would be for Stefan to think of training to be a doctor.

But I'm happy to be a nurse. Medicine is too academic for someone like me.

In the dimly lit church Stefan prayed for the patients he would look after that day. He prayed for Martha and their newborn daughter, and for their friends. Then he got up and went outside. He paused beside Leo's grave to light the first candle to burn there on this first day of little Rianna's life. As it burned he prayed for his daughter, and, this time of Christ's Passion, he remembered the words, 'Father, forgive them,' and prayed for those killers of Leo who had shown no pity, whose trial would be carefully stage-managed in front of multi-national media. Everyone knew that however stringent the penalty meted out to the killers might be, once the media had turned its fickle spotlight away from Koravia, the terms of their sentences would be whittled away.

Yet what was the use of politically loaded judgements? Compassion was what counted, the compassion of Christ. That was what Leo would have wanted for his killers; and that was the meaning too of at least some of the flowers and candles on his grave.

Let your kingdom come to us in Koravia.

Stefan turned away from the graveside and went off to work, leaving one small flame burning in the first dull light of day.

Four days after Easter Thomas borrowed a car from friends and drove Stefan to hospital to bring Martha and Rianna home. They found the table set with Easter cakes and candles, while Joanna and Maria were busy in the kitchen among mouth watering smells.

'Welcome home to you both,' said Maria.

'Please let me hold Rianna,' begged Joanna. 'Oh, she's beautiful.'

'She's much tinier than Niki was when Helen brought him home, but she's got far more hair. Look at her curls. Oh, shsssh now Rianna, it isn't time for you to wake up yet. Look what a good girl she is. I just said "shssh" and she shut her eyes at once!'

'Long may that last!' Rianna's grandmother observed.

The doorbell rang. It was Andrey. 'Christ is risen!' he greeted Martha.

'Christ has really risen,' she replied, returning the threefold kiss. 'Oh, what's this, Andrey?'

'Just something for our goddaughter from both her godfathers,' Andrey said. 'Thomas and I went shopping yesterday.'

'And you actually managed to find a beautiful quilt like that in Koravia!'

'Not in the shops, of course, but we knew where to go to get it made.'

'Tell Martha about the telegram,' interrupted Joanna, who was still admiring the baby.

'Telegram?'

'From Michael, Helen and Niki,' said Stefan. 'It came today. I sent them a telegram to tell them about Rianna.'

'Let me see it. Oh, listen everyone: "Welcome Rianna and congratulations to Martha and Stefan. May the risen Christ fill you with his love. Michael, Helen and Niki." How nice that it came today, though it's funny that their telegram got through when their letters don't. Perhaps things are changing that way too. But where's our little daughter? She ought to be in bed. Do you think you're going to like your crib, Rianna? There. Let's dim the lights. After all there are candles on the table. I'm sure Rianna won't mind the sound of our voices. It was a whole lot noisier in hospital, I can tell you,' Martha added as they gathered round the table.

'Is there any news of Elizbeth these days?' she asked as they ate their meal.

'You knew that Elizabeth met Helen at one of her concerts?' Thomas said. 'I think Helen helped Elizabeth when she was going through a bad patch. It seems she actually stayed with Helen and Michael for a while.'

'How nice that must have been,' Martha said, 'like a little bit of home when you're abroad.'

'Perhaps. Anyway the good news is that Elizabeth plunged herself back into her flute playing. She phoned us yesterday to say that she's won a scholarship.'

'That's good.'

'Yes, but wait till you hear the rest,' put in Stefan. 'The scholarship is with a really well known flautist, Maestro Marcellino.'

'I'm sorry, Thomas. I'm so ignorant, that name doesn't mean anything to me.'

'It wouldn't have meant much to me either if I hadn't heard Elizabeth rave about him,' Thomas admitted. 'But the thing is, he's done arrangements of Koravian folk tunes, which won him the Friend of Koravia award a few years ago.'

'So this puts Elizabeth back in favour with our regime, does it?' asked Martha, as she ate cucumber salad and chicken with relish. 'This is delicious, Matusha.'

'Joanna was the cook, not me,' her mother-in-law said, 'but if you'll allow me to say so, I'd go easy on those cucumbers, Martha, in case they upset Rianna.'

'I've noticed already that what I eat affects her,' Martha said. 'Would you excuse me? I must go and have a look at her. I keep having to have little peeps, just to make sure she's really there. In hospital I lay for ages just looking at her.'

'Let me share her as well, then,' said Stefan.

'We'll excuse you both while Joanna and I bring up the next course,' his mother said, stacking plates together.

Andrey gathered bowls and cutlery. 'I'll help you take these downstairs,' he offered, and at that moment the doorbell rang again.

'What a noise, and Rianna hasn't even noticed.'

A neighbour tapped on their door. 'It's someone for

you.'

'I'd better go.' Stefan detached himself from the corner where his daughter lay in a wooden crib.

'Flowers for Mrs Martha Cornelius!' A girl in the uniform worn by shop assistants stood on the doorstep.

'That's my wife. Who can they be from?'

'There's a card inside.'

'I see. Thanks very much.'

He ran upstairs. 'Flowers for you, Martha.'

'For me! What an enormous bouquet! How beautiful! Whoever can have sent them? No one's ever given me flowers before. I feel like an opera star, or something.'

'Oh, Martha, I should have sent you flowers in hospital. I'm sorry.'

'You gave me a flower – Rianna. Though it was hard work getting her out. Anyway, you gave me snowdrops once.'

'So I did! Still, come on, let's see who these are from.'

'See that, he thinks I've got a secret admirer!' Martha opened the wrapping. 'Freesias and narcissi, and Easter lilies, as well as flowers I don't even know the names of. But who could have spent all that money on me?'

She unpinned a card. 'Oh, Stefan, Matusha, look.'

The card simply said, Congratulations, George.

'Your brother? Oh!'

There and then in the midst of the Easter meal, while her guests shared traditional Easter cakes, Martha wrote a note to her brother-in-law.

Dear George,

Thank you for those gorgeous flowers. I'm so thrilled with them that I'm writing at once before anyone has even put them into water, which your mother is just taking them downstairs to do. I want you to know that your little niece is looking forward to meeting you, and your sister-in-law would like to get to know you too. Thank you again and lots of love from Stefan and Martha.

'This has got to be the nicest Easter ever,' Martha said.'

'I agree,' said Stefan. 'Thank you all very much.'

Later that night when their guests had gone home and Maria and Joanna were asleep, Martha fed her daughter. Stefan encircled them with a protecting arm. 'Who would have thought a little new life would bring so much joy?' Martha said softly.

'Yes, but it's not just us and our baby daughter either,' said Stefan, 'It's everything. It's Koravia too. I mean, in spite of Leo's murder we all hope that we have reached a turning point – in fact, it might even be the murder which got us there. The dark times are ending. There's a new day ahead.'

Some other Swift Books you may like to read. . . .

Bright Dawn is the third in a trilogy about Stefan. The other two books are *Dark Journey* and *Light Sentence*.

Dark Journey
Jenny Robertson

Stefan pulls down a flag as a gesture of defiance and is sent to a labour camp. On release he is called up for national service and drafted to a prison punishment corps. Here he is given a special assignment – a prisoner, Michael, who changes his whole outlook on life. From then on Stefan is in danger, but though the journey may be dark in places there is new light ahead.

Light Sentence
Jenny Robertson

Stefan meets Thomas, who is involved with producing Christian literature secretly. Stefan joins the underground printing outfit and helps to get news of the oppression in Koravia to the West through a tourist. The authorities wait for a suitable opportunity to pounce. Stefan and Michael are arrested but their trial is an expression of light for Koravia.

Sky High
Veronica Heley

Chrissy thinks she is a mess and that her busy, efficient parents don't love her. She daydreams of a world in which she is always popular and successful. One day she takes a short cut into this world. Could it really be bad for her when it makes her feel so good?

Mirror Image
Gail Vinall

A group of five teenagers form a Christian rock band. They have high hopes of success and do well in their competition. The test comes when there is a conflict of loyalties in the group and they are forced to reconsider their image.

Joy in the Morning
Carol Marsh

Kate looks back sadly at the happy times she spent with her father. She blames her mother for his death and cannot forgive her. Darren seems to understand her but he has his own problems at home and decides to leave. He wants Kate to go with him and the more she thinks about it the more Kate feels that would be the solution. But then Darren disappears and the situation changes.